A FACE IN THE LEAVES

NINA ORAM

LUNA NOVELLA #8

www.lunapresspublishing.com
ISBN-13: 978-1-913387-81-5.

For Annette, for your Art that continues to take my
breath away, the ghosts and graveyards,
the walks and English Folklore, Kate Bush
and Chubby Bunnies.

Big thanks to Luna and Joe, but special thanks
to some of the many women who inspire me;
Francesca, Coirle, Kathryn, Adri, Annette, Mum,
Sam, Shell, Helen, Denise, Jo, Emma, Alexa,
Barbara and Susan.

Contents

...

Stood in the sprawl of the city, it's hard to imagine the land as it was once. Lush, green ferns mirroring a soft, whispering canopy so huge it had seemed to go on forever. Or the hush, the quiet, low hum of the forest, so different from the noise of people and the harsh, metallic screech of traffic.

Not much left now. Just pockets, small patches on the edge of the city parks, and the infamous stretch of forest where murderers go to bury their dead in the warm, scented earth. No one tells you, but it's not a recent thing. They've been burying them there for centuries, for millennia, giving them up like a prized offering to some pagan God. A God of the woodland, of the brown, rough bark, and a myriad of green, streaked with falling sunlight and snatches of darkness. And oh so silently, the forest takes them. Nestles them to its dark, earthy breast and devours them. Slowly, gradually, until the flesh, and then the bones, rot down into the rich, carnivorous soil.

But sometimes it wants more, demands more, than an offering, or a gift, and becomes the place of the hunt. An accomplice, helping the murderer to chase down his victim, tripping them with open, knotted roots, or bamboozling them with twists and turns and clusters of oak trees, of birch, beech and ash, dusted with patches of nettles and bindweed, that all look the same. Rarer still, it needs no one to do its killing, and hunts and murders alone.

Without meaning to, she slipped down, until she was half-sitting, half-lying against the trunk of the oak, her chest whistling. Already, they were coming for her. Slipping over one another, their numbers growing and swelling, as they slid across the ground towards her.

Exhausted, the last of her energy spent, she gazed up into the dark, almost empty branches and, listening to the creak of wood, and the low, quick rustle, waited for them to come.

Chapter One

It started with Ben, or rather, that's when her involvement started. The first time she met him was at the community art centre and gallery where he had his studio. In London, using a car seemed almost criminal, so she took the Tube to West Green, then the bus. The centre bordered Hornsey, the less salubrious cousin of Muswell Hill and Crouch End, but only just.

She was doing pieces for one of the city papers on young artists, the city's up-and-coming talent. He was the last of five and, in her opinion, the best. Working in black charcoal and pencil, with thick, angry strokes, she'd never seen so much fury on a canvas so devoid of colour. And yet, it was more than that. Just anger would have been a cliché, the alienated young man, projecting out into the world. No, it was the softness, the warmth he'd put into the landscape, affection tinged with sadness, and a strange longing, as if he were painting the face of a love he'd felt but had never really had.

The centre was in a converted Presbyterian church. Red brick, build some time in the Victorian era and from the outside, it looked like just any other converted church. A sandy coloured plaque had been built into the wall, just over the door. Erected in eighteen hundred and eighty-five by Ezra Pennyworth for the people of Hornsey. Ironic name. The surname inverted; he obviously was.

The door was open, the entrance a porch with another door. Stepping inside and past a noticeboard filled with brightly coloured local adverts that reminded her of community centres in the seventies, she opened the second door, and stopped. *Nice.*

Converted into a hall long ago, with a wide, rectangular space and parquet floor, it had been converted again and, with a ruthlessness that was almost shocking, someone had cut a line through the centre of the roof and filled it with huge windows. Light flooded the room and found its way into every corner, every space. Kept polished, the parquet floor gleamed, the oak wood made an even deeper, warmer brown by the white walls. They'd created a reception area in the corner to her left, using a counter, a hip height horseshoe in fake wood, and three chairs. Horizontal to the counter, in the far corner, a small café served just drinks and cake, surrounded by comfy-looking chairs and seat bean bags. Next to it was a small play area for the kids, with a boxful of toys, and a square green mat that made her think of the reading mat in her primary school.

Rich, colourful art filled the walls, some of which was surprisingly good, some of which was atrocious, the artists not having even the faintest idea of how to draw shape, texture or even perspective. The local art group, she guessed. Still, it showed an inclusivity, even if it did hurt her eyes and make her wince. But on the whole, it was a nice use of space; modern, but with a nod to its heritage.

"I'm here to see Ben Lewis," she said to the receptionist.

Blonde, young, with a loose orange and green square top, slipped off a white, infinitely smooth shoulder, she looked like an artist roped in to hold the fort.

"Oh, right. I think he's here, somewhere," the young woman frowned. "Probably in his studio. I'll try his mobile."

Picking up the phone, she stared at a list of numbers sellotaped to it, in a way that made Lily think this must be her first time.

"Don't worry. Just tell me where to go, and I'll find it."

"Okay." Putting down the phone, she indicated, using her hand, like a blade. "If you go through the double doors at the end and into the corridor, you'll see a door opposite. Go through it, then left. Then first right. That'll be the studios. Ben's is the third on the left."

"That's great. Thank you."

She cocked her head, as if remembering something. "Could you sign in?" She pointed to the book left open. "It's for fire regs."

"Of course."

Using the pen attached to it with string and another piece of Sellotape, hastily applied, Lily did as she asked. Stretching over, the woman looked at her name upside down.

"Lily Goodfellow." Her eyes widened. "The Lily Goodfellow?"

Lily suppressed a laugh. Said like that, the young woman made her sound like a foundation or an arts prize. "You've heard of me?"

"Yeah, every art student's heard of you. All the well-known art journos were men, until you. And you're here to see Ben?!"

Lily leant forward, confidential. "I'm looking to do a piece for one of the big newspapers, but it's not certain. You won't tell anyone, will you? I don't think Ben would want anyone to know."

She shook her head vigorously, like a child. "No, of course not."

Her face was too unusual to be pretty, but she was striking, with her open, friendly way that wasn't at all self-conscious. Lily imagined she was very popular with the lads. Or girls, she corrected herself immediately.

"And you say you're an artist?"

"Art student. Just started my final year. But I share one of the studios with a couple of people."

"If you give me your name, I'll look out for you."

"Really!" She flushed, her cheeks going a classic rosy pink. "Amelia Brown."

"Amelia Brown. I'll remember that name. Amelia Brown. Good luck with yer final year, Amelia."

Lily left her and, conscious of her gaze, walked towards the far double doors. It was impossible not to be flattered by her reaction. Very rarely did anyone know or recognise Lily outside of exhibitions or openings. But, putting her ego aside, it was even more gratifying because it was so vital that all young artists, not just female artists, saw the opinion of women as just as important as those of men. Like everywhere else, the art world was still hopelessly male-dominated. Just as it was rich and white. But it's changing, a British-Asian colleague had told her the other night at an opening. *Yeah, right,* Lily had snorted to herself, inside her head, as she'd quietly sipped her wine. Like the rest of society, the art world does just enough. Admits just enough to counterattack anyone who shouts, and then closes ranks again. And even those admitted never, ever, get to the inner sanctum. There's always some excuse, some reason. She should know. A woman *and* working class, originally from a rough council estate in Reading. But maybe, she countered, I'd been in the business too long, I'm becoming beyond cynical.

She went through the double doors and into a narrow corridor. With toilets to her left and a small kitchenette to the right, she went straight across, through the door and into a modern extension. Wide, with a high ceiling, the walls to the corridor were white, and the carpet a soft grey. Handrails ran along both walls, like the rails on a track, the light wood mirroring the doors and the skirting board. Left, Amelia had said. She went left. The corridor was quiet, and the doors firmly closed. There was no one else here, and no sound coming from the rooms as she passed. She went through another double doors, and saw another door, into another corridor. That must be it.

Without carpet, this space was more basic, and immediately she could smell paint. She passed two doors, one right and one left, and glanced through the glass. Studios. Definitely the right place.

The door to the next studio was open, and one glance at the pictures within told her it was Ben's. She was about to go inside when a man appeared at the far end of the corridor, stepping out of a room. It was him. Lily recognised him instantly from his last exhibition. They hadn't met, and she hadn't gone up to introduce herself, but she'd seen him talking to a small group. Dressed in jeans and a dark, bottle green top, he moved swiftly towards her.

"Can I help?" he called, in a deep, North London accent.

"It's Ben, isn't it? We spoke on the phone. I'm Lily Goodfellow."

He covered the distance in three bounds.

"I'm sorry, Miss Goodfellow, I didn't recognise you from over there. I'm Ben." Smiling, for a moment, he hesitated, as if he wasn't sure what to do, then held out his hand. "I would've collected you from reception if I'd known you were here."

She took it. "Lily. I like to find my own way. It's an unusual building."

He was very good-looking, with black hair cut short, and brown skin, but his eyes were beautiful. Deep brown, they sparkled with a light, an energy that came from within. If she were young, single and prettier, she'd probably follow him around like a lovesick puppy. Almost immediately, she wondered what Amelia on reception made of him. Together, visually at least, they'd be some couple.

"Yeah. This new bit was added about five years ago. Behind the church was an old derelict factory. The owner sold it, and everyone thought, y'know, they'd knock it down and build luxury flats or something, but it was bought by a local businessman who wanted to do something for the community."

"And he built this?"

"He gave the council the land on strict conditions, and helped with the funding, but most of it came from fundraising and other local businesses."

"Impressive. Although, I think I remember something

about it. Didn't he pay for a new mosque as well, around the same time?"

"Just the roof. The old one was leaking." He indicated with one hand. "This is my studio. Would you like to see it?"

Lily grinned. "That's why I'm here."

His answering grin was embarrassed. "Yeah, right, of course."

He led her inside and, without a word, she walked past him, taking it all in. It was unusually neat, his equipment and materials carefully stacked. Or maybe that was for her benefit. Medium-sized, with large windows running the full length of one wall, his work filled the other walls, and the myriad of stands placed on a long table. A closed laptop sat on a small desk, and in front of that was a small square table with two chairs. His empty easel and stool were next to the windows, to get the best light. Two more stands stood between the desk and the window, and she recognised the pictures on top, two from his exhibition, but the rest were unfamiliar.

She knew he was watching her. Trying to gauge her reaction, although she was too professional to give anything away so easily. She wondered idly what he saw. An older woman at the top of her profession, chic and timeless, with thin, iron-grey hair cut in a blunt, expensive bob, and casually dressed in designer cut-off jeans and wedge shoes and a light cotton top. Meryl Streep in *Mamma Mia*, only without the dungarees (she wasn't skinny enough) and the long, honey-blonde locks. Or an ageing journalist, vain and conceited, trying desperately to stay young and hip.

"Would you like a drink? We've got tea or coffee, or water?"

"Coffee would great, thanks. Black, one sugar."

"Okay. Back in a sec."

He left, and immediately she began moving from picture to picture, taking her time. Attached to the wall, in a long, rough line, they looked strangely like a forest, as if she was standing in front of one, facing the first line of trees, but in miniature. This forest was dying, slowly disintegrating from right to left, one picture at a time, until the last landscape, burnt and scarred by pollution, was nothing but a wreck, a post-apocalyptic nightmare. Doing it this way was surprisingly powerful, like a watching a human life slowly fading. That simile was too close; it reminded her of Marjorie, and she forced her mind to focus.

Now, these images, were they inspired by the same place, or possibly imagery? The woods and forests in his mind's eye, an amalgamation of different places, rather than one distinct reality. It was something to check. And another thing, standing all together, she could see the pattern, the way his art had been developing, its driver. It was a rage slowly building, becoming darker and darker.

She moved to the two easels, and the first of the paintings she knew. Large, it was a small copse of trees, their verdant, green forms reduced back and back, like legs, with the layers of skin slowly peeled off, until those in the centre resembled bones.

Something caught her eye, near the edge of the picture. It was a tiny face, peering out of the foliage, its eyes just two black circles. She leant in for a better look. Nothing. It wasn't there. Or rather, she was too close to see. She pulled back, but she still couldn't see it, so she cocked her head, thinking it was the angle. No, there were no circles, no tiny black eyes, just the lines of the trees and the shades of light and dark. She'd made a mistake; her brain had taken the shapes and made its own interpretation. She frowned. It wasn't like her – she did, after all, make a living out of studying art, its minute detail – but then, anyone could make a mistake. She moved to the second picture, just as Ben reappeared, carrying a mug and a tall, metal water bottle.

"I hope I've made it strong enough," he said, bringing it over the table.

Reluctantly leaving the picture, she joined him. "I'm sure it will be fine."

It looked strong. Sitting down opposite him, Lily dropped her bag on the table and took a tentative sip.

"Tastes good to me."

"Great." Looking relieved, he yanked off the top of the water bottle and took a swig.

"Are you ready to start?"

"Yeah, I think so."

"There's a way I like to do it. Firstly, I've prepared some questions," she explained, rooting into her bag. "I'd like to know more about your background, your influences, that sort of thing. Ah hah!" She pulled out her phone. "Do you mind if I record it?"

He shook his head. "No."

"Great." Pushing her bag away, giving herself room, she began tapping the screen. "It makes life easier, and it means I can listen back to what you say. But just so you know, no one else will hear this. It's completely confidential. Data Protection and all that."

He nodded, but in a way that told her he'd agree anything

she said.

"I must warn you; I usually like to do a second interview. It gives me time to digest, and I can come back with more questions."

"Yeah, fine, whatever."

"Good. Now, ready?" He nodded, and leaning forward, she pressed the button.

They went through the usual stuff; his family, the early days, how he got into art. His mother was white, born in Hackney, and worked as a community nurse, and his dad was black, an engineer from Nigeria. Doing well at school, if it hadn't been for a change in his art teacher, he'd probably have gone down the scientific route, following his father into engineering. But thankfully, the new art teacher had recognised his potential and worked hard to foster it. God bless the good secondary school art teachers, Lily thought. Over the years, how many kids had they helped to steer towards their true calling?

She leant forward. "Your work, it's all about climate change."

"Of course. I mean, what else is there?"

"But does that worry you? I mean, I know it's the single most important issue for humanity, but everyone else is doing it. Aren't you worried that you'll be lost in the crowd?"

She watched his neck stiffen, the only sign that what she'd said had affected him. But if she'd made him angry, she was glad. She *had* been in this business too long. And didn't want the usual spiel, the advertising, the *I believe in this so passionately* crap. She wanted to get to the real artist, the person beneath. Wanted to know what drove the fury that leapt out of the canvas at her; threatened to rip out her throat.

"Yeah, but I suppose we all come at it from at different angle. I mean, how it affects us personally, and our relationship with nature."

"Yeah." She resisted the temptation to tell him how many times she'd heard exactly the same thing, almost word for word. *Our relationship with nature*, blah, blah, blah. No one talked about nature's relationship with us. Or rather, its complete indifference to our thoughts and feelings, our rich, poetical outpourings. "Aren't you worried that people will turn off? That it will become just more of the same?"

"There is a danger of that. But hasn't art always been like that? The main themes of the times, or the style, the fashion."

"That's true. Although, there are always trailblazers, the people that set the trend and the theme."

"Yeah, but I don't think artists work in a bubble; we influence one another and inspire each other with our work. Look at Van Gogh and Gauguin, or the Beatles."

She cocked her head, surprised, and a little impressed that someone his age knew enough about The Beatles to reference them. "A fan, are you?"

"Me mum is, and listening to them since I was a kid, they sorta stuck."

She made a mental note, then continued the discussion. "But surely climate change supersedes all that? It's not just the theme of our time. With the potential to end human civilization, if not the species, it's the final theme. Finito."

"All the more reason why we'd be compelled to show it, surely?" He rejoined, flashing her a grin. "As I said, what else is there?"

She laughed. She liked his cleverness, and without him

realising, it gave her an insight into the way his mind worked.

"There's so much in climate change, so many things you could show, but your work centres on trees and forests. Why is that? Why them particularly?"

Lifting the bottle, he took a long swig. "I suppose for two reasons. As a kid, I was fascinated by trees. They just seemed so big, so wide, and tall, reaching high into the sky. And old, wise." He looked inwards, his eyes glazing. "The wise, old oak. The healing ash. Every country, every culture has folklore around them. To our ancient ancestors, they were a magical, wonderous thing, and I can't imagine a world without them. I don't want to." His eyes cleared. "They were vital for our ancestors. They got so much from them. Sometimes, I think, on an instinctive level, they understood far more than us, how vital they were; that's why they revered them. We've all heard the rate of destruction of the Amazon rainforest, but no one, apart from conservation groups and activists, talks about the destruction of European forests. And yet, every tree, every wood or forest we destroy, brings us a step closer to our own destruction. It's hard not to think we deserve it for not having enough respect."

"Is that where the anger comes from? Your love of trees and your awareness of what we're doing? Your earlier stuff is less…visceral. Softer, more sentimental, and by default, more traditional." It sounded like a slur, even though she didn't mean it as such. "Was that a conscious change?"

He looked away. "I guess. The more aware you become, the angrier you get, the more passionate."

He was holding back. She knew it, felt it instinctively, although she couldn't quite figure out why. Maybe young, eager for success, deliberately, or possibly subconsciously, he was giving answers that he thought would please her, or wouldn't offend anyone. She asked more questions, designed to get him to relax, and it worked, to a point. She'd long ago decided that most artists and creative people were the same. Once you start them on their creations, you couldn't shut them up. Ben was interesting, though. A conundrum. He sounded open, and listening to him talk, he didn't seem angry. He'd probably be disgusted at her for thinking it, but he just seemed a nice lad, thoughtful, and… positive, so positive. He really believed people would stop climate change. Surely, this was passion, belief and commitment, and the very opposite of the terrible, burning rage she saw? Or was that it? Was she back to the same feeling, that he trying to modify or suppress his rage and ironically hide the very thing that drew her to his work?

"The inspiration for your images, where do they come from? Are they from one particular place, or from across the country, or countries?"

"They're from a few places. Woods and parks around North London. This whole area was part of the Ancient Forest of Middlesex, which covered most of Middlesex, North London and parts of Hertfordshire. Now there are just these tiny patches left. Like the Amazon, I wonder if our ancestors thought they could cut, raze and burn, and it, too, was endless, limitless."

"Interesting." She'd heard this before, but not in any detail. Another mental note; this one to find out more about London's ancient forests, because it would make good background. "Well, I think I've got enough for the moment," she said, switching off the microphone.

"Oh, okay." He looked disappointed, as if he felt he was only just getting into this stride.

"I want to process this."

And think of a way through his armour. She might be an arts journalist, but she was still a journalist, with a journalist's instincts and a nose for a story. And there was definitely more to his work than he was showing her.

With a couple of quick taps, she went into her diary. "So, I'm looking at when we can meet again. Next week, preferably." She scrolled through the week, searching for a free space. "Hmm. Could you do Tuesday afternoon?"

"Yeah," He answered straight away. "What time?"

"Half two?"

He nodded.

"Good." She added it.

She'd have to work over the weekend, but with the deadline close, Veronica would be on her back, and she needed to get it finished.

"Do you know when it'll be in the paper?"

"To be honest, no. You're my last interview, but the whole thing has to go through my editor, and there are no guarantees."

"I understand."

Again, he looked so disappointed.

"But we'll keep in touch, and I'll let you know," she reassured him. "And she doesn't usually say no. Well, not often."

He smiled at that, but she knew he'd be on tenterhooks until she called, and she couldn't blame him.

*

Leaving him in his studio, she saw herself out. The café closed, the hall was empty, including the reception; there was no sign of Amelia. Through the porch and out onto the front step, she closed the door behind her.

It seemed to take forever to get home. A delay on the tube meant Lily was stuck, in between stations, for almost twenty minutes, although at least she was sitting. Even worse were the crowds when she had to change, with too many people squeezing into the narrow underground tunnels and too few trains taking them away. Squished against the wall at the back of the platform, any more pushing, inadvertent prodding and knocking and she felt like her head would explode. Thick, sticky, red; there was a perverse satisfaction in the thought of her blood and brains splattering the other passengers. This was another thing she was getting too old for. Too crabby, too impatient, with a new streak of viciousness that made her worry she was developing the dreaded sharp tongue of her grandmother.

And the internal combustion engine puffing away in the centre of her didn't help either. Hot, sweating in more than this inexplicably hot weather, all she wanted to do was to get home and have a cold shower. Sighing, keeping her arms carefully down so as not to inflict her body odour on the other passengers, she closed her eyes and willed herself away. Out from the noise and the crowd, and into a soft, cool forest, the ground dappled with sunlight. And quiet. It would be beautiful and peaceful, with none of Ben's primeval rage. Maybe, when it came to her turn to retire, they could move to the country. Somewhere near a forest, or the sea, her hot body blasted with cool, Channel air.

Two more trains came and stuffed now into hard, rattling metal. She swayed and lurched with the carriage, the only thing holding her upright the sweating bodies around her. Thankfully, it wasn't far. Just three stops, and a short walk, and she was back home a little after five. Closing the door behind her, Lily let her bag drop.

Almost immediately, Jeremy called from the kitchen. "How did it go?"

"Good."

She paused, debating whether to go and see him, or go on upstairs for that shower, but too late. The kitchen door opening, he shot down the hallway, towards her.

"I need a shower," she said quickly, holding him off with both hands. "I stink."

"What's new?" He grinned, ignoring her hands and hugging her anyway.

"What have you been up to?" she asked as soon as he let her go.

"Out in the garden. It's beautiful out there."

He'd retired a little over six months ago, and unlike his closest friend, who'd retired just after him, he loved it. Didn't feel bored, or useless, or any of the things other people complained about. He had so many things to do, so many interests. She was almost envious of his quiet, steady routine, and the way he ambled through it. No, that wasn't quite it. Pottering. That was the word, and he embraced it, in a way only he could. His days seemed to pass in pottering happily from one thing to another. Cooking, baking, stopping for a coffee and a read of the paper, then out into the garden, a snip here, a snip there, tidying, pruning. Or out, for a walk in the park, or to the local market or book shop for a browse, and another stop for coffee, and maybe a slice of cake.

Watching him, admiring, she wondered if she would retire as graciously and be able to fill her days with such small, seemingly inconsequential little things that would make her feel so happy and contented. But she doubted it. She knew she was a restless soul. A fidgeter, like a child jiggling from one foot to the other; always looking for the next thing, and even when she had it, never, ever, feeling fully satisfied. Bored now. They should put that on my gravestone, she thought, wryly.

"Come and join me, after."

She did as he said. Had her shower and changed her top and, feeling better, stepped out of the kitchen and into the sunshine. Jeremy was sitting at the bistro table, reading a library book on native flora.

"You sit down," he said, putting down the book and jumping to his feet. "I'll make you a drink."

"Thanks, darling. I could murder a cup of tea."

She sat. In the last six months, Jeremy had transformed the garden, showing an enthusiasm and talent no one, not even his brother, Anthony, had suspected. In Lily's head, there had been nothing wrong with it. It may have been a little boring, grass with a border of shrubs and the odd flower, but it was easy to manage and took little effort or thought. But now he'd turned it into an oasis. An orgy of texture and form, interspersed with flashes of deep vibrant, or pale delicate, colour. Small trees had been strategically placed to give them the best light, and them, the best view; Willow and Acer, Magnolia, and fruit trees, pear, plum, apple and olive. Around them, he'd placed shrubs, Fiji Cherry, Mexican Orange, Butterfly Bush, Australian Bottle Bush and Hebe; purples and reds fizzing. Next came the grasses, ferns, long stems and soft, narrow leaves swished gently in the wind. And then flowers; reds, blues, purples, oranges and yellows mingling in a riot of colour.

She didn't know all their names, just the ones that appealed to her, but Jeremy did. Just as he knew exactly the best spot to put them in, and what height they grew to. He knew because he'd researched it all so carefully. He'd tried to tell her, and she'd tried to listen, for his sake, and because he'd worked so hard, but to be honest, she didn't really care. Just seeing the result of what he'd done was enough. Her life's work had taught her she didn't need to be able to create a masterpiece to admire one. Or to sit in it, sipping wine.

"Here ya go." He was back with a chilled glass of white wine in both hands, as if he'd read her mind.

"Wine! What happened to the tea?" she asked, even as she took the glass.

"I thought you might need this."

One sip, and she sat back, enjoying the feel of the wine as it cooled her insides, all the way down. "Mmm, it's perfect. Thank you."

They smiled and clinked glasses.

"So, it went well."

Lily took another sip and, with a conscious effort, put the glass down. Suddenly, she wanted to savour it, and this, sat in the warm, late afternoon sunshine, talking with Jeremy. The first week in October, this must surely be their last one before the errant autumn finally arrived, looking red and flustered, like a new student who'd got lost on their way to their class.

"Yeah, I think so. He's very interesting."

Jeremy laughed. "That good-looking?!"

"Oh, yes," she agreed. "Definitely. But cautious. I can't get into his head. I'm going to interview him again, but I need to think about it if I'm to get a better insight."

"Well, you always do. It's what you're known for." He looked down at his watch. "I'd better get the dinner started."

She straightened. "Oh, you're not staying out here, with me?"

"I won't be long," he reassured her, standing up. "Once dinner's in the oven, I'll be back."

"What is it?"

"It's a surprise. I found a new recipe, so you'll just have to wait and see."

Giving her a quick peck on the lips, he went inside, and Lily took another sip before putting the wine down, glass on glass scraping.

She gazed into the shrubbery. Although it was obviously a trick of her eye, she could still see the face in Ben's picture staring back at her through the foliage. Just like a Green Man. A Green Man. It was a strange thing for her to imagine. Like something you'd find at Glastonbury, it wasn't her style at all. Didn't they have them as garden plaques? Nailed the head to a wall, or the trunk of tree.

"Well, that's that." Jeremy said loudly. "It took longer than I thought."

Starting, she blinked rapidly. Her head felt woozy, as if the wine had gone to her head, or she'd got too much sun. She glanced at the glass and saw there wasn't much gone.

"Are you alright?" Jeremy asked, touching her arm.

"Yeah, I think so." She rubbed at her eyes. "Just tired."

"I'll get you some water. I didn't think…in this heat."

"No, it's okay. I'm fine, really."

Reluctant, he sat.

"That was quick," she said, then, to change the subject.

"What was quick?"

"Whatever you're cooking."

He gave her an odd look. "I was just saying it took longer than I thought. Almost half an hour."

"Half an hour?" She rubbed her eyes again. "I must've fallen asleep."

"Maybe you should take it easy tonight, and get an early night."

"Nah." Picking up her glass, Lily smiled at him over the rim. "Got work to do." She took a sip, ignoring the disapproving shake of his head. "Nice wine. You should get that again."

Chapter Two

Searching for London's ancient forestry proved to be more time-consuming than Lily imagined. She was hoping to find a website that gave her the full of history of the forest that had once covered most of north Greater London, but it wasn't that simple. Instead, she found herself exploring the existing forests, woods and parklands and working back. She pored through their websites; Ruislip Forest, Horsenden Hill, Highgate Woods, Queen's Wood, Coldwell, Bluebell and Scratchwood. She scrolled through pictures of trees of all shapes, sizes and hues; photos taken at dawn, dusk, with the sun lifting or lowering, in the first flush of spring, or lush, verdant summer. Sweeping or choking, empty and quiet, or filled with running, laughing kids. The remnants of the ancient forest were everywhere.

According to the records, it had been vast in Saxon times, stretching from Bow, of the famous bell, to Uxbridge in the west and Potters Bar in the north. Watling Street had been part of an ancient trackway that had cut through the forest, and run all the way from Wales to Dover.

There had been other forests too, with the Forest of Essex

to the northeast, deforested down into the Royal Waltham Forest, before being deforested down again into Epping Forest. And to the south, the Great North Wood that had stretched from Deptford on the Thames and out to Croydon.

Who knew, but way before the Saxons, and the Romans, the whole area could have been one giant forest, reaching down to the marshy plain of the Thames, its body cut in two by the river. It was hard to imagine. Hard to imagine all those buildings, streets, houses and people, all gone.

It was late when she finished. She could understand Ben's fascination. She'd never thought that a gentle stroll or walk, in a London wood, was like reaching back into an ancient past. Into a time where it was the trees, and the forests, not humankind, that dominated the land.

*

The week slipped into the weekend. Sunday morning, and with the sun shining, Lily got up early and rattled off her review for the night before and emailed it to Malcolm, the arts editor of a city paper. She'd been at the opening night of a new exhibition in a gallery on the South Bank, called "Disappearing Worlds", featuring five artists from the Maldives, Brazil, Australia, Norway and the UK. It had been a good night. For the first time in ages, Jeremy had come with her and, to her delight, they'd spotted her old friend Toby and his Spanish wife, Lucia. He was a food critic and she a restaurant owner, who, in Lily's opinion made the best tapas in South London.

After the opening, on impulse, the four of them went on to a nearby Spanish bar Toby knew, sharing olives, salted almonds and a rich, scented jug of Sangria until one in the morning.

"Just don't tell anyone," he'd laughed, his eyes twinkling, as he'd ordered a second jug. "I've a reputation to maintain."

He might laugh, pull the piss out of food snobbery, but Lily knew he took food and wine, and his reputation, very seriously.

*

Her review sent, Lily would have gone back to bed if Jeremy wasn't already up and making breakfast. Her head was still fragile after last night, and she didn't like to admit it, but she couldn't remember getting home. Her last memory, they were in the back of a taxi, the driver moaning about something, but she wasn't really listening, but after that, nothing. Instead, she had a shower, but the water was so hot it made her head swim.

In the kitchen, she drank a full pint of water, and then they ate breakfast with the sun streaming through the window. Around it, the morning sky was already a deep, glorious blue.

"Do you fancy a walk?" she asked, sipping her tea.

"I thought you wanted to go into town?"

"I've changed my mind." She didn't think she could bear even the smaller Sunday crowds. And besides, a walk would do her good, the fresh air blowing the hangover away like cobwebs.

"Have you any ideas?"

"Yeah, Highgate Wood."

She'd dreamed of forests and woken up thinking of Ben's work. What could be more perfect than to walk in a remnant of his ancient, giant forest, and one of the places that had inspired his work? They'd been there a few times, and it was a beautiful wood, filled with tall, broadleaf trees. And autumn was the best time of year; swishing through crisp, brown leaves, shin-deep, with the strangely enticing scent of death and dying filling your nostrils. And after, with your face flushed and tingling from the cold and the exercise, a quick drink in the local; dark, with old musty furniture and a red carpet, acrid with the aroma of spilt warm beer. Of course, there would be no carpets to swish through yet; the leaves had only just begun to fall, but the wood would be full of colour, the trees' canopies bright and burnished, with gorgeous autumn hues.

On the way over, the Tube was quiet, the tiled walls echoing; just as she liked it. It gave her the same feeling as late at night, as if London belonged to them. Sat next to Jeremy, any longer and she'd've fallen asleep with the sound of the tracks and the slow rock of the train. But the journey was too quick. Just half an hour later, they stepped through the park gates, past a line of dog walkers, and into the wood.

Even with the good weather, some of the trees had begun to drop their leaves, as if they knew the season, not by the weather but by the days, like humans do. High in the sky, the sun flashed through the branches, dappling the ground with light and turning the yellow leaves into golden. Lily sighed happily. No wonder Ben was making them his life's work. It was impossible to walk here and not feel it lift your spirits, even when you didn't think they needed it. Although, of course, that wasn't only what he saw. There was that dark, burning rage too.

Across a break in the trees, a group of teenagers were

sitting on the grass, under a huge ash. One shouted, and another screamed, their voices echoing, making everyone turn. Towering over their heads, the ash, with its thick, almost puffy canopy, like dark green clouds, reminded Lily of a child's drawing. It must be very old. She studied its form, its lines and shades of colour. After Ben's work, it was like seeing a tree for the first time. She was surprised how much it was affecting her; she couldn't seem to stop thinking about it, the pictures lingering, like the scenes of a film that both disturbs and enthrals.

"I think I will get a dog," Jeremy said suddenly, his voice thoughtful.

Lily dragged her mind away. It must have been seeing the dog walkers. He'd been talking about getting a dog ever since he retired, but hadn't yet made up his mind. She didn't help. It was totally his decision. The dog would be his, and his responsibility. It would be him walking it in the cold and the rain, or when he was too tired or too lazy, not her.

"I'll get a rescue one. Will you come with me?" he asked.

"If you like. But like I've always said, it's up to you. I won't have much to do with it."

He laughed. "You talk tough now, but as soon as you see them, looking up at you with their sad eyes, you'll crack. And knowing you, you'll go for the saddest, the loneliest and the most unloved. That's you, Lily; all hard on the outside, but inside, you're as soft as butter."

"Then we'll see, won't we!" she laughed back. And then, she realised what he'd said. "What do you mean, hard on the outside?!"

He grinned, his eyes sparkling. He'd been waiting for that.

Had said it deliberately to get a rise out of her. "Figure of speech."

"Typical man, mistaking strength in a woman for hardness!" She sped up, pretending to be angry, the movement making her hips sway.

"Aw, Lily, don't go," he called, laughing.

"I'm not," she shot back, over one shoulder. "It's just you've got too slow, old man!"

"Old man?! Old man?!" He began to run.

Giggling, she ran too, but slowly, and it didn't take him long. Catching her around the waist, he pulled her to him and they kissed.

"Jem, I do love you," she cried, throwing her arms around him.

"I love you too."

Another kiss, and they continued, arm in arm. Ahead, a young couple was standing, watching, on the edge of the path, and Lily gave them a mischievous grin. You don't have to be young to be madly in love, to play fight, and kiss and cuddle in public, she thought gleefully. Us grey-haired wrinklies can do it too, even after so many years together.

They walked deeper into the wood, following the path as it meandered through the trees, crossing other paths. The deeper they went, the quieter it got, as if most people stayed around the edges. The sky had clouded over, the sun disappearing behind the thick grey, making the wood colder and darker. Just in a t-shirt, Lily's arms began to goosebump.

"Hold on." Jeremy stopped and, bending down, began to tie a loose shoelace.

She ambled on, keeping warm but giving him time to catch

up. The wood was wilder here, dense, more overgrown and less well-kept, with stinging nettles and tangles of bramble. To her left, a tree had fallen and was leaning drunkenly against a neighbour, its trunk covered with ivy. It was hard to believe they were in the middle of a city, with people, roads, shops and houses not so far away.

A breeze ruffled her hair, caught the edge of the trees, and they murmured softly, leaves rustling. Grown too close together, the vegetation in between the trunks spilled into one another, separated by small patches of darkness. The leaves rustled again. There was something in there. A bird, maybe, a pheasant, or a rat? Lily moved closer, but too thick; it was impossible to see. A tree creaked and, instinctively, she looked back at Jeremy. He'd finished tying his other shoelace and was getting to his feet. Another gust of wind, another rustle, and the tree creaked again. She thought she heard something scamper, and leant forward to look. Another gust, this one so cold it must surely be coming down from the North, from Greenland or the Arctic. She rubbed at her arms and, staring into the undergrowth, thought how quickly the atmosphere could change without the sun's warm rays.

"It's getting cold," Jeremy said loudly, walking towards her. "Autumn's arrived with a bang."

"Yeah, it feels like it."

Glancing over at him, something moved out of the corner of her eye, and she followed it between two trees.

"What the—?!" She took a step back.

"Lily?"

She blinked. It was gone. Apart from the undergrowth, the gap between the trees was empty.

"I thought…I saw something."

"Where?" he asked, coming close.

"There." She pointed. "I didn't really see it. It was just a glimpse."

Leaning forward, Jeremy peered into the undergrowth, about a metre and half off the ground.

"Maybe it was a bird?" he suggested after a moment, straightening.

"I guess."

She'd only seen it for a split second, but it didn't look like a bird; it looked like a face. The face attached to the eyes she'd seen in Ben's pictures, the same size as a human head, but low down, as if its owner were bending.

Jeremy frowned. "Lily, are you feeling alright? You've gone pale."

"I'm fine." She wiped stray hairs off her face. She'd seen hatred in those eyes, and Ben's terrible burning anger.

But she couldn't have, for there was no face, no eyes. It was just her imagination; she'd been thinking about his work, hadn't she? And she was tired, hungover. Had stayed out too late and drunk far too much for her poor body, more than she'd done for quite a while. Suddenly, the walk in the wood didn't seem like such a good idea.

"I'm starting to get hungry," she conceded.

"Low blood sugar. Should've brought a snack."

It was a good point. Tired and hungry, and dehydrated, no wonder she was seeing shapes in the trees. She'd be seeing dots next, or flashing lights.

"Too late now. We can get something after the walk."

He looked at his watch. "Half one. Not too bad."

They continued. The footpath turned into a wide arc, and she looked back, just once, at the place she'd seen the face. Of course, there was nothing there; just trees and vegetation.

They turned the corner, and immediately, the sun came back out, its light catching the edges of the leaves. It should've made the wood feel better, like it had before, but somehow it didn't. It still felt cold and dark, unwelcoming, as if her first feeling had been a mask, a show, and this was the wood's true self. But a wood didn't have a true self, it wasn't a being, an entity – it was a collection of trees, a landscape.

"Lily, what's the rush?" Jeremy asked suddenly. "Are you that hungry?"

Unconsciously, she'd sped up. "Actually, I need the loo," she lied quickly, unwilling to admit her own silliness.

With a stretch of his long legs, he matched her speed easily. "You're falling apart! Can you hold on, or maybe stop, go behind a tree?"

"No, I'll be fine. I'm not getting incontinence just yet!"

They continued, not speaking, both lost in their thoughts. Walking fast, it wasn't long before they were back in the busier part of the wood. With more people, it felt better now, more normal. Following the signs, they went around the playing field to the café and toilets. Called the Pavilion Cafe, because it was situated inside an old cricket pavilion, it was complete with red brick and tiled roof and a madly overgrown wisteria. Outside was full of young families, but inside was much quieter, and they managed to find a table next to the window.

"You're looking brighter," Jeremy commented as, her lunch finished, Lily downed the rest of her water.

"I just needed to something to eat."

It was true, she did feel better, much better. Around them, the room was getting busy, as those finishing their walk came in for afternoon coffee or tea and a slice of cake. An old, white-haired couple wandered around with a tray, looking longingly at their table.

"We should go," Lily said, spotting them. "I think they want our table."

They got up and, catching the man's eye, Jeremy pointed downwards, indicating the table was free. But even then, they almost weren't quick enough, as a bullish-looking man with a tray appeared from Lily's right. Automatically, she sat back down again, just as the old woman bounded forward. Her white head down, like the cab of a juggernaut dusted with snow, she was too fast, unable to slow. She hit the table, knocking it and Lily's chair back with a scrape so loud it seemed as if the whole room had turned to look.

"I'm sorry," she said, her voice cross and her face red and flustered. "But are you going?"

The bullish man had gone.

"Yes…I was just sitting back so he…" Lily's lips twitched. It seemed useless to try and explain. She stood up again. "Yeah, we're going."

"You shouldn't've sat back down," Jeremy laughed outside. "It was like musical chairs. I'd've liked to have seen which one won."

"No contest. That tray of his would've gone flying, like my chair."

They laughed together.

"What do you want to do now?" he asked as they went back towards the entrance.

"Go home, have a snooze."

"There's a match on later. I might wander down, see if it's on?"

He was asking if she minded. "If you like. I'll probably fall asleep in front of the TV anyway."

*

Later, with Jeremy gone, she sprawled out across the sofa and tucked the cushion under her head like a pillow. A Cary Grant film was on the TV, an old black-and-white madcap comedy. Normally, this would be a treat, a reminder of the winter Saturday afternoons she'd spent as a kid, watching TV matinees with her sister, but today she was too tired. Drawing up her knees, she pressed her face into the cushion and closed her eyes.

*

She was running, her breath coming out in short, shallow gasps. Soaked, her hair plastered to her face; around her, the trees shook and writhed, pounded and battered by a storm. Coming from behind, the wind shrieked as it whipped through the branches and tore down the path towards her. Catching her shoulder, it pushed at her, forcing her on like a giant hand. It caught the leaves underfoot, too, and they gushed away from her like the torrent of a river. There was too much noise; she couldn't think with the shrieking, creaking and rustling that sounded as if the whole forest was alive, and coming for her.

Her foot slipped, and she fell backwards into soft, springy

moss, her body bouncing once, twice, before settling. Laid on her back, her face open to the sky, she looked up and the forest came in on her, the leaves, ferns, branches and trees falling on her like the pack of cards in Alice in Wonderland. Like Alice, she was fighting and shouting.

She woke with a jump, the dream instantly forgotten. The room lay in shadow, the sky outside dark. She swallowed; her mouth was dry. The film had finished, and two men in suits were sitting opposite one another, talking seriously. Levering herself up, she rubbed at her face and checked the clock. Six. Jeremy would be back soon, and it was her turn to cook. Sleeping had been a bad idea. Instead of feeling better, she felt worse, her head fuzzy. Getting up, she threw her arms into the air and stretched. Then padded out, through the hall and into the kitchen.

Chapter Three

Tuesday afternoon, the weekend already a distant memory, and it was her second meeting with Ben. Amelia wasn't on reception this time, it was an older woman, who seemed far more confident, more efficient. Once more, Lily signed her name, and once more, she moved through the old church hall and the back corridor, then out into the new building.

Like the last time, Ben's studio was empty, the door half-open. About ten minutes before two, she was early so, thinking it would give her time to look again at his work without him, she slipped through the door.

The sky was overcast, from rain that had only just stopped, but even without the sun the area near the windows was bright. The other side was dim, the walls and Ben's pictures shaded with a light grey shadow. It gave the room an odd, surreal look; like the merging of two photos, one new, sharp, overdefined, the other aged and blurring, fading towards sepia. And it was quiet. Quieter than she remembered, the hush unnatural, as if not just the room, but the whole building, had been emptied of people, then enveloped, cocooned, in thick clouds of wool.

Moving to the table, she placed her bag on top of it. She

rolled up the sleeves of her cardigan then, hands on hips, turned and faced Ben's pictures. After yesterday, they were no longer just trees, but the silent, unmoving ghosts of those in Highgate Wood. The hairs on her arms lifted, and it was just her imagination, but for a moment, she thought she heard a bird, twittering, the sound echoing against the hard, paint-splattered floor and the stark white walls.

This fancifulness was getting her nowhere. Pulling down the sleeves again, she walked over to the pictures from his exhibition. Immediately, without even having to search, she saw the tiny face in one of the canvases.

"I don't believe it," she muttered, with a glance towards the door, half-expecting Ben to appear.

When he didn't, she cocked her head, exactly as she'd done the last day, but this time… Disbelieving, she moved sideways. It was still there. Moving back, she stared intently at it, not just waiting but daring it to disappear. Almost completely covered by foliage, its eyes peered out from behind a trunk. The last day, it had come and gone so quick, she'd only glimpsed it, but now…it had to be a Green Man. What else could it be? She'd never seen one drawn like that before, with an expression of such hatred and malice. She could almost feel it, coming out of the paper at her. Ben was even better than she'd first thought. Strangely chilling, unsettling, it was quite a feat to get so much feeling into such small lines.

She moved to the second picture. It took her a few seconds, then she spotted it. On the opposite side of the painting, like a mirror image. It had to be some kind of optical illusion. Half hidden, like a primitive Where's Wally. But why bother? For what purpose; unless, possibly, to unsettle the viewer even further. Or make them question themselves. An optical illusion done well, it could be another Escher or Duchamp, but it was a risk and could easily pull his work into the cheesy or the faintly comical.

She thought of his other pictures. It wasn't there last week, but what about now? Starting near the door, she began to move slowly along the wall, her eyes fixed on the canvases. There, on the right side, and there, in the centre. She shimmied sideways. Going slowly, taking her time. It was there, and there, on the left, near the edge. It was so strange. She was seeing it so easily, whereas the last time there had been no sign. Unless it was the difference in the light from the overcast sky. She moved to the next picture. There it was again, just on the edge, as if the trees on Ben's canvas were real, an actual forest, and the face was inside, slipping around the trunks and through the undergrowth, moving from picture to picture, following her.

Her disquiet building, she reached the far wall. The tiny face was in all of them, its expression never changing, as if Ben had taken all the anger and rage from his pictures and crystallised it into the not quite human face. Inwardly, Lily shook her head. No, that wasn't right. It was more, the feeling that the face, the Green Man, was the channel, the focal point of a rage that was already there. A thought occurred to her. What if it wasn't in all of them? What if it was following her, and she ran back to the first picture? Too fast; it could still be making its way across and might not be there. What would she do if it wasn't?

"Miss Goodfellow, you're here already!"

Jumping, Lily whirled, her hand going to her chest. Peering around the door was Ben. Pushing it open fully, he stepped inside, and she saw Amelia behind him.

"Lily," she replied automatically. "I was early, so I thought I'd come on in. I hope that was okay."

"Of course."

They looked at one another. It had to be trick, an illusion, she thought, glancing sideways at the pictures. She was silly to get so rattled.

"Hello, Miss Goodfellow," Amelia smiled, looking embarrassed. "We met in reception."

"Yes, of course," Lily replied, flustered. "How are you?"

"Good."

"Do yer want a coffee?" Ben asked.

"Ah, no, thanks." Lily shook her head. "I've two cups already today."

"I should go," Amelia said quickly. She touched Ben's waist. "See ya later?"

"Yeah."

Bending down, he kissed her lightly on the lips.

"Bye," Amelia gave her a small wave.

"Bye, Amelia."

Another time she'd've been delighted to be proven right. As Amelia disappeared, Lily walked unsteadily back to the table. Turning on the light, and closing the door, Ben joined her. They settled themselves.

"How was your weekend?" she asked, mainly for something to say. Behind the casual professionalism, that was almost a refuge; she was deeply shaken, not just by what she'd seen, but what she'd felt.

"Okay."

"Were you busy?"

"Nah, not really."

She took out her phone and laid it on the table. Her hands, she noted, feeling curiously detached, were steady.

"She's a nice girl." He looked at her quizzically. "Amelia."

"Yeah, she is. Are you ready?"

He nodded, stifling a yawn.

"Keeping you up?"

"Sorry." He straightened, and gave her a weak smile. "I'm just tired. Had a late night."

"Okay, then, let's get started."

She pressed start on the video, and started with the question utmost in her mind, but still trying to keep it casual. "Tell me, I'm curious about the face. What made you do it? At best it should be an unnecessary affectation, or indulgent, absurd, fantastical; at worst, a weak, amateurish error, but it's not, it's…unsettling, and if I'm honest, a little creepy. How did you do it? Some kind of optical illusion, I suppose?"

His mouth had fallen open; it took him a minute. "W-what?"

"The face. I suppose it's meant to be a Green Man. It's on your pictures. I saw it last week, just for a second, on the two from the exhibition, but then it disappeared. But now it's there again."

He was staring at her as if she'd lost her mind.

Annoyed, she tutted impatiently. "C'mon, I'll show you."

Turning off the video on her phone, she got up and went over to the easels, Ben following.

"Look, just there," she pointed, triumphant.

"Where?" He stooped, for a moment obscuring her view.

"Not too close. You did it, you must be able to see."

He stepped back, and she looked again. It wasn't there.

"Maybe I'm not looking in the right place. Maybe it's the angle." Gently pushing him to one side, she stood square onto it. "I can't seem to see it." She tilted her head left, then right. Took a step back, then forward. Nothing. "I don't understand."

"What?" Ben asked. "What you looking for?"

She ignored him, and turned to the second picture. "Maybe this one."

It wasn't there either.

"But –?" Flummoxed, she looked between them. "I don't understand; how are you doing it?!"

"Doing what? I'm not doing anything."

She gestured angrily. "Making them appear and disappear, like some stupid bloody magician!"

She marched over to the wall and stared hard at the nearest picture, checking the whole surface bit by bit. It wasn't there. She moved to the next, and the next. Nothing.

"Appear, disappear? What are you talking about?" His eyes narrowed. "What do you think you saw?" he asked carefully.

Don't look at me like that, she wanted to scream, I saw it. "I told you, a face! Covered with leaves and foliage. A Green Man. Technically, you'd just drawn a pair of eyes, the rest was…implied by the foliage around it. But it was definitely a face."

"So, a couple of dots?"

"No, not dots, circles, eyes, *eyes*. It was there, I swear. They were eyes…only." She stopped. There was nothing on any of them that remotely looked like part of a face. "It was the same last week. I saw them, then suddenly they were gone. As if they weren't there."

"You must've made a mistake. I didn't draw eyes or a face."

Something in his voice made her look at him. He shifted uncomfortably. He was lying, she was certain of it. This time there was no mistaking what she'd seen. But why was he lying?

"Shall we continue with the interview?" he asked, quickly changing the subject. "If you want to."

"Of course I want to!" she snapped.

He was patronising her, treating her like a doddery old woman, when she knew exactly what she saw, only there was no way to prove it. She took a deep breath. Calm down, Lily. It wasn't like her to lose it with people, especially those she was interviewing. She was a professional. "Maybe I will have that coffee after all, if you don't mind."

Could she have made a mistake? Could it be like in Highgate Wood, and a trick of the eye? No, way, she thought, rejecting it, this wasn't a blink of an eye. She knew exactly what she saw.

"I'll get–" His phone rang, and for a moment, he looked like a man reprieved. "Hold on."

Pulling his phone out of his back pocket, he turned away before answering.

"Hello, hello. Oh, mum. Look, I'm busy, I've got…What – what? I can't hear you. What about Dad?!" With a sigh, he turned back, and moving the phone away from his ear, half-covered it with his hand. "I'm gonna have to take this outside, the reception's really bad–"

"Go on," she interrupted him with an impatient wave. "I'm fine."

"Okay, thanks." He shot out of the door, as if he couldn't wait to get away.

She heard him in the corridor, shouting into the phones, telling his mother he had to go outside, GO OUTSIDE; his voice slowly fading. Silence.

Immediately, she went back to the easels. Was he trying to make a fool of her? Get one over the renowned Lily Goodfellow? Scare the shit out of her and get her to put something ridiculous in the article, then do a big reveal afterwards? It seemed unlikely. And besides, he didn't seem the type to be so vicious.

She studied both pictures carefully, examining every inch of the canvas. This wasn't the usual way optical illusions worked; once you saw them, you couldn't stop seeing them, but this one seemed to be able to come and go completely. But how? How did he do it? Maybe there was more to this than clever art. Carefully picking up one of the pictures, she hefted it, then turned it around. It was just a usual back, nothing out of the ordinary. She turned it back, traced the ink lightly with the tips of her fingers. It was just ordinary ink. Nothing special. Replacing it, she took a step back and frowned. Her initial idea had been the light, but the sky hadn't changed; it was still overcast. And then she remembered; he'd put the light on. It must be that. Darting over to the switch, she turned it off, then dashed back. It made no difference. No trick of the light, then.

Defeated, she was returning to the chair when she noticed a portfolio file leaning between the desk and the wall. It was probably empty, but you never knew. A quick glance at the door and, grabbing the file, she laid it on the table and undid the zip. What exactly she was looking for, other than more work, she didn't know. Maybe inside the other work there would be some sort of clue… Opening it like a book, she saw drawings, on A4 paper, the top edge serrated as if they'd been torn from a sketchpad. Pushing them carefully onto one side of the folder, she began to go through them, picking them up one at a time, before placing them, facedown, on the opposite side. Small, drawn in charcoal and pencil, they were rough, unschooled, and she guessed these were his very early work, when he was a boy. She could imagine him, sat somewhere, one foot on top of his other leg, making a triangle with his upper leg, using it as a rough easel for his pad. Mostly of nature, they were even more sentimental, although very nicely done. She turned a scene over.

Underneath were a couple of portraits. A woman, possibly his mother? There was a likeness. She spotted the edge of another scene and pulled it out. In colour, it was a view from a hill, out across a park. Drawn in autumn, at the base of the hill, trees lined the path. Two or three deep, native, and foreign, deciduous and evergreen, they mingled effortlessly. Their canopies were splashes of deep reds and purples, burnished golds and oranges against the green and the grey. Very beautiful, but not quite as interesting, artistically speaking. But there was no sign of the face. She picked up the last one, and saw two envelopes, brown, A4, tucked, overlapping, into the mesh sleeve of the folder. Both worn and creased, they looked old. Feeling like a thief, but full of curiosity, Lily pulled out the top one, and folding back the flap, peered inside. Another drawing. Very carefully, she pulled it out.

It was very amateurish, as if the lines had been drawn too fast and too carelessly. But there was an atmosphere to it, a sense of…she shook her head. Full of raw talent that possibly, one day, would lead to genius. It was good when really it shouldn't be. It was a drawing of a park. In the centre, a woman walked across grass, a wood behind her. It was late autumn, judging by the leaves on the ground and the empty branches. Surely, it was the same park as in the other picture? And what was that, in the trees? Dropping the envelope back into the file, Lily held the drawing in both hands and peered intently at it. It was the face again, the Green Man, only this time the dark, ancient eyes weren't glaring out at the world, they were glaring at the woman. Burning, searing a hole into the back of her head. She'd found it. There was no mistake.

"What are you doing, touching those?! They're private! I never said you could look at them!" Ben cried from the doorway, the hand holding his phone hanging down.

He leapt across the room towards her. Too stunned to react, all she could do was watch as he threw his phone on the table, snatched the picture out of her hand and, dropping it into the file, pulled the two sides together. Hands shaking, he tried desperately to zip it up, but it kept slipping.

"Here, let me." Calmer than she felt, Lily grabbed the ends and held the file still for him.

To her amazement, he dropped it and flopped down in the seat opposite. She'd thought him angry, but she was wrong. He seemed, if anything, shocked and dismayed, and was it her imagination, a bit scared?

"I'm sorry, I didn't mean to upse…to offend you."

He pressed his hand to his forehead. "You didn't offend me. It's just no one's ever seen that before."

Standing, very gently, Lily opened the file just enough to find and pull out the drawing. "How old where you when you did this?"

"Fifteen."

She sat down. She had to be careful, or he would clam up. Be gentle, Lily, she told herself. Don't push, coax.

"It's very good. Unusual. It has an atmosphere. A feeling of a place much older. Who's the woman?"

His eyes slid away. "I didn't know her. She just happened to be coming out of the trees when I was drawing it, and I sort of included her."

Ignoring the face of the Green Man, she looked at the woman again. She couldn't really see her face. He'd smudged the pencil, almost as if he'd deliberately wanted to obscure her features, but there was something familiar about her. Her coat, maybe? Or the way her hair hung across it, and the trousers, wide above the knee but tapered in at the ankles, as if she'd seen her in a photograph, wearing exactly the same clothes.

"She seems very familiar, but I can't quite put my finger on why. Is she famous?"

"No, not in the way you mean."

Lily cocked her head, thinking. "Wait a minute…"

He pulled himself upright. "She disappeared. It was on the news."

For a moment, she couldn't quite get it, then she remembered. It was years ago, but for days, the woman, and the photograph, were everywhere.

"Yeah, that's right, I remember. Anne something. One day she just vanished. There was talk she'd been murdered, but they never found a body." Her eyes widened. "When did you draw this?"

"Two days before. I won't ever forget it. Me dad was watching the news, and summat made me look up… and I saw her on the TV. Her photo." He shuddered. "She looked just the same. Was even wearing the same coat."

She looked at the picture again. She couldn't expect him to understand; it had obviously been traumatic for him, and by his reaction still was, but to a journalist, this could be gold dust. Anne Darrow, that was it. Her name was Anne Darrow. She lived alone, and was a bit of a loner. Ben was probably one of the last people to see her alive.

"What's the name of the park, again?"

"Wettin. Wettin Park."

Ah, yes, she remembered. A small, obscure park no one had really heard of until Anne's disappearance. In north London, surely it must be another part of Ben's lost Forest of Middlesex.

"Are you sure you didn't know her? I mean, to draw her like that. Was she a friend? Someone you knew, just from the park?"

He sighed and ran his fingers through his hair. "Like I said, I didn't know her. I only met her once, when I did the drawing. But she was nice. Kind."

"What happened?"

"Nothing really. She saw me drawing and came over. Normally I wouldn't let anyone see a drawing before I'd finished, but I'd drawn her, and I suppose I felt I kinda owed it to her."

"What did she think?"

His eyes glazed, as if he were remembering. "She liked it, at first." He blinked and his eyes refocused. "I've never told anyone exactly what she said, not the police, or my mum or dad."

It was her turn to stay silent. She knew if there was any

hope that he would tell her, he had to come to it in his own time. But this was the crux of his work, she was sure of it. And then, just when she was sure he had decided not to tell her, he began to speak.

*

Even as a kid, I mostly drew nature. I wasn't confident doing people and I preferred to be outside, trying to capture what was going on around us, mostly unnoticed. I used to go to the park a lot, because of the trees, and because you could sit there for hours and no one would say anything. And there was always something to draw, especially with the seasons. But I suppose I liked autumn the best, not just the colours, but the feel of it. I think even now, if I went to live somewhere hot, it'd be autumn I'd miss.

I don't know if you've been there, but the north entrance to Wettin Park opens onto the hill. The main path goes across the top then down, winding to the left as it follows the shape of the hill. But before the brow of the hill, to the right, coming off the path, is a grass track. If you follow it, it leads you into the small wood and out the other side, where it rejoins the path just below the brow. I was sat on the park bench there, facing the trees. It was the first time I'd sat there. Normally, I sat further down, so I could see the views. You can see the whole park from there and the city around it. I drew that so many times. Me mum's got one on her wall. There's one in the file; I did with colours.

I was drawing the wood when I noticed her come out. Not many people go that way, so I thought it would be good to include her. I had to be quick, so I just did the outline and finished it later. I was so busy I didn't realise she'd seen me, until I looked up and saw her standing there.

"Hi," she said, smiling.

"Hi," I answered.

I was embarrassed. You know the way kids are when an adult they don't know speaks to them. But I didn't like to show it.

"Your drawing?" she asked.

I nodded, being polite, when usually I'd been sarcastic. Y'know, to give the impression I was hard, even though I wasn't at all. But I don't think I thought about it at the time, I just responded. But there was something about her, as if she needed me to talk to her. As if, at that moment, she didn't want to be on her own.

"What are you drawing?" she asked.

"The woods. And you."

"Me!" she laughed, delighted, and her whole face lit up like it was Christmas. "Wow, I've never been drawn before. Can I see?"

"I don't like people seeing. Not before its finished."

Her face fell. "Oh, I see. I'm sorry."

Seeing her disappointment, I felt bad. She'd looked so happy.

"Yeah, okay," I said, relenting.

I held it out so she could see; as she bent over, long hair fell over her face. Dragging it back, she held it tightly in one hand.

"It's very good," she said, eventually looking up. "You have talent."

I squirmed, caught between delight and even more

embarrassment. "Thanks."

"Would you like to be an artist?"

"It's all I've ever wanted."

"Then you will be, I've no doubt. I'll have to come see your work when you're famous."

I laughed, thinking that would never happen. There was a silence. She straightened, and for a moment, I thought she was going to go, but she seemed to change her mind.

"Do you know this park very well?" she asked suddenly, hovering.

"Yeah, me mum used to bring us here, when we were little, innit."

"That's nice." She looked back at the wood. "I'm new here. Been here just a few weeks, but already I've grown to love this beautiful park." Another look back, as if she wanted to talk about someone, but didn't want them to hear. "Have you noticed that not many people walk in the wood?" There was a pause. "Do you know why?"

"No."

"No…stories or legends? I mean, just about the wood, not the whole park."

It was a strange thing to ask, but she seemed so nice, and I dunno, I suppose I felt sorry for her. She seemed very lonely.

"Me mate, Andy, reckons it's haunted, but no one listens to him. He makes up a lot of shit."

"Haunted? By what?"

I shrugged. "I dunno. He reckons he was in there, one time, sat, having, y'know, a spliff. He heard something behind him, and when he turned round, he saw—"

She leant forward, ever so slightly too close. "What?"

"He said he didn't see it properly. It was just out, y'know, the corner of his eye. But he said it looked like a tree, only it was moving." I laughed. "I told him he'd had too many spliffs, innit, but he wasn't having it. Like I said, he makes up shit. He can't help it, he's an arsehole."

"I thought he was your friend."

"Yeah, he is, but he's still an arsehole."

"But–" She stopped, and I could see her thinking. "There must be something. Someone must know something." She fixed her eyes on me. "Are you sure you there's nothing else?"

"No, nothing." I shifted, wishing she would look away.

As if seeing my discomfort, she smiled, but in the way people do when they're not really feeling it. "Well, I better go. Thanks for showing me your picture. You've made my day, knowing that I'm in it."

Tilting her head, she took a last look at my drawing, and then, with a cry, jumped back.

"Are you okay?" I asked in alarm.

"Yes, yes," she cried, her eyes wide, backing away. "I have to go."

I watched her go, glancing fearfully at me over one shoulder. I was so confused, but then, I looked down at my drawing.

*

He fell back, as if telling the story had exhausted him. Maybe it was just the relief of finally getting it out. There was a pause.

"Do you know why she was so interested in the wood?"

He shook his head. "No, she never said. I thought at

the time she was just lonely, or sad, but now I think she was scared."

Lily frowned. "Scared of what?"

He wouldn't meet her eyes. "Of something she saw in the wood."

Lily looked at the picture with the face staring out of the wood, burning a hole in the back of the woman's head, and suddenly she knew what that something was. "You saw it too. The face."

He didn't answer.

"That's why you draw it. That's why you keep drawing it."

"I didn't. I don't."

"You didn't what?"

"I didn't see it in the wood. All the time I was drawing, it wasn't there." He saw her look of incredulity and leant forward. "I'm not lying. I didn't see it!"

"It's okay," she replied quickly, lifting her hand, trying to placate him. "I'm just trying to understand."

"And I didn't draw it, either."

She laughed at that. "So, what, someone else did?"

"No, no one added it. It's all my work. Those are my lines, only…I didn't draw the face." He gave her a doubtful look. "You won't believe me."

It was on the tip of her tongue to say he'd started now, he might as well finish, but she knew better. "Maybe not deliberately, but subconsciously?"

"No." He shook his head. "I'd know, I'd see. I never draw it, it just appears. Like it did that day. When I first showed the woman the picture, there was no face. I know because I didn't draw it, and she didn't see it. But the second time, she saw. That's why she reacted like she did. And afterwards, when she'd gone, I looked and there it was."

"And now?" She could feel herself staring, but she couldn't help it. Was he seriously expecting her to believe this?

"It's always there. You can't always see it. Sometimes I don't see it for days, or weeks, but then it reappears. But I didn't draw it, I swear," he said desperately. The bright light in his eyes had gone, replaced by something dark and burning. He looked… haunted.

Her first thought was that he needed help. That it was a shame; he had so much talent, but sometimes there was a thin line between talent and… but then, she'd seen it too. There must be another explanation.

"So, the face is in the other pictures?"

He nodded. "Yes."

"And it appears and disappears?"

He nodded again. "Yes."

"Do other people see it?"

"I don't know. No one's said anything before."

So, she was unusual. Distinguished. Lily frowned. She didn't believe it. It was like a con, with the conman making the mark thinking there was something special about them. Appealing to their ego. Why didn't he just admit what he'd done? Optical illusions in art were perfectly fine, especially one as clever as this. There was no need for trickery, pretending there was some supernatural cause to it. Of course, it was a way to get his name known. If she wrote this, everyone would want to come and see his work, if only to see if they were one of the special ones that the Green Man appeared to. It was certainly ingenious, but it was also dishonest, and ultimately self-defeating. Because how could the art world ever take him seriously after that?

He leant closer; the look on his face intense. "You have to believe me. I don't draw it."

But she couldn't. Faces don't just appear in pictures. They're drawn, even subconsciously. And yet, she'd seen for herself, how it appeared and disappeared.

"Okay, say I believe you. Why do exhibit your work if this face keeps appearing? Why do you keep drawing the same thing; woods and trees?"

"I didn't think anyone else saw it. I thought it was just me." He hesitated, and she had to admit that it did make sense. "And I've tried to do other work, other things, but it doesn't work." He shook his head. "It always comes back to trees."

Like being stuck in a loop of endlessly repeating trauma.

"You don't believe me. You think I'm ill." There was a pause. "You're not going to do this, are you?" he asked, but it wasn't a question.

"What?"

"The interview. The piece on me, on my work."

He looked so devastated, close to tears, as if his whole world had come crashing down on top of him, and she couldn't help but feel for him. She thought of what Jeremy said about the dogs. Maybe he was right, and she was soft after all. Soft as shite, she told herself sourly. But she had her reputation to maintain, and she couldn't be associated with anything approaching deception. The art world had a very long memory and, unsurprisingly, those at the top didn't take kindly to anyone who made them look like gullible fools. But what if he was ill? What if he was doing all this unconsciously, and there was no deliberate intent? Could she walk away from him for that?

"I don't know," she admitted. "But if I did, and I'm not saying I will, but if I did, I wouldn't mention the face. In fact, I want nothing to do with it."

"I don't want you to! If you hadn't asked, I'd never have told you. I don't want anyone to know! I don't even want to think about it, ever!"

She wasn't expecting that. He sounded so genuine, his anger and his words heartfelt. Surely, if he was trying to con her, this was the last thing he would say? It made her think he was genuine, and really didn't know what he'd done it. And besides, she couldn't help it; she liked him, and didn't want to believe that she could've got him so wrong.

"Why don't we take a break? You've had a shock and I…I don't what to think. What if I go and make us some drinks? It'll give us both a moment to calm do... breathe."

Pushing back the chair with his legs, so that it scraped loudly, Ben stood up. "No, I'll make it."

"You don't have to. I'll–"

"I know where everything is," he interrupted, his voice shaking. "And I need the air."

"Okay, then."

In three long strides, he was across the room. Yanking on the door, he threw it open, then closed it behind him. It looked as if he was going to slam it, like an angry, petulant child, but at the last moment, as if he'd thought better of it, he pulled it gently to.

Lily breathed out. That went well, she thought, ironically, glancing down at the picture. The face really did give her the creeps. And if Ben's story was true, it was a very strange coincidence that Anne Darrow had disappeared two days after she'd seen it. If what he said was true. Which really wasn't very likely, unless you believed in dark, vengeful wood sprites. She studied the line of the trees again. Even if he didn't remember, how had he done it? How did he make the face appear and disappear? Then, suddenly, out of nowhere, she remembered the second picture.

She had to be quick – he wouldn't be long, and she really couldn't afford for him to catch her again. Their relationship was almost in tatters already. A quick glance at the door and, lifting one side of the portfolio, she thrust her hand inside the webbing. She felt the end of the envelope and then, pulling it out, let the file drop. Another glance at the door, she folded back the flap. Feeling inside, she pulled out another piece of sketch paper. This side was blank, so she turned it over.

It was a pencil drawing. Basic, with light shading. A woman lay at the foot of an oak tree. On her back, with one arm out flung, her eyes and her mouth open, the later hanging loose, the captured stillness to her body could only mean one thing. She was dead. Something was in her mouth, filling it so completely that the edges were tumbling out across her face and down onto her neck. Lily squinted, looking at the shapes. They were leaves. Someone had filled her mouth with leaves; pressed and stuffed, until they'd suffocated her.

"Oh my God!"

It was Anne Darrow. It had to be. Ben had seen her lifeless corpse and drawn it. Only, no one knew for certain she was dead; she just went missing. No one but Ben. Lily went cold. For a moment, she let herself think the unimaginable, then she was pushing it away. He was just fifteen when she disappeared, for Christ's sake. A kid, a boy. There had to be another answer. She looked at the door again. He'd be back any minute. Her heart thudding, she grabbed the envelope and tried to stuff the picture inside, but it wouldn't go. Her fingers were shaking too much; the edges kept catching. Another glance. She was wasting precious seconds. Dropping the picture, she thrust her hand in the envelope, widening it. Now it would go. She tried again, and this time, the picture slid smoothly inside. Pushing down the flap, she slipped it back inside the mesh and, closing the file, laid it back down. Her heart still pounding, she picked up the first picture and tried to relax. Only just in time. The handle pressed, and the door swung open.

"I made you coffee. I hope that's okay," Ben said from the doorway.

"That's great. Thank you." Even to her, her voice sounded a bit breathless. She swallowed, making a show of looking at the picture.

There was something about the drawing of Anne Darrow, even seen from a distance, that didn't look right. She frowned, but there was no time to figure out what it was. Ben was at the table.

"Thank you," she said again, taking the mug from him.

He gave her suspicious look, but didn't say anything as he sat down opposite. There was a pause.

"I'm sorry I got angry," he said eventually, not looking at her. "It was just, y'know, the shock. I haven't seen it for a while, and I thought it was over, but this has just brought everything back."

"I understand."

He shook his head. "You don't. You can't understand what it was like. Even before I started seeing…y'know…I was just a kid, and seeing her on the news, and knowing I was one of the last people to have seen her before she disappeared, it was traumatic. The police interviewed me and everything, in case there was anything I remembered. Then at school, all the kids wanted to know. Everyone thought she was dead, even though they never found her body, and the other kids kept on and on about it, but I wouldn't tell them. I should've. Should've told them lies, anything to shut 'em up. I thought they'd get bored, and give up, but they didn't. In the end, it became like a game."

Lily shifted, uncomfortable. She was one of the lucky ones, that had never really experienced bullying, but she'd seen it happening to others. Kids, when they started, could be as vicious as they were relentless. "How long did it go on for?"

"I left school the next summer. I was supposed to stay on, do my sixth form there, but I went to the local college instead." He shook his head. "A couple of kids from my year went, and I thought it would start up again, but it didn't."

"It must have been tough, Ben. I'm sorry. I didn't mean to bring it all back."

Maybe this picture was his way of dealing with the trauma, by putting all his child's fear and horror into it. Didn't psychologists do that with traumatised kids? And, like he said, even at the time, it had seemed that Anne Darrow was most likely dead, so it wouldn't take much for him to imagine it. But then, she argued back to herself, it wasn't easy to capture the body in death, to make it look like the person was dead rather than sleeping.

She had no choice. Veronica was waiting, and realistically,

she didn't have time to go elsewhere.

"D'you know, Ben, I think I have enough."

"Enough? D-Does that mean you're still doing it?"

"Of course. But we won't mention the face, or Anne Darrow."

"That's what I want," he replied eagerly. "My work's about climate change, nothing else."

"And you're right – it belongs in the past, so we should leave it there." She put her phone in her bag, and picking it up, got to her feet. "The deadline's next Friday, so hopefully I'll be able to let you know sometime the week after."

"Great." Joining her, he looked like a condemned man who'd found himself with an unexpected last-minute reprieve. "Thank you…Lily."

"I wouldn't thank me just yet. Let's see what my editor says first."

They shook hands, in a strangely formal gesture, as if they were making a pact.

"I'll see myself out."

Chapter Four

Jeremy was out for the evening when Lily got home so, making herself a tea, she took it straight upstairs with her to her office. There was so much to think about, but first she needed to get the article done, while it was fresh in her mind.

Concentrating, she didn't notice the evening drawing in, or the house growing cold around her. Hollow, empty, without the sounds of Jeremy downstairs, the shadows crept slowly from room to room. Lengthened the stairs, and the pins of the balustrade, as they edged silently upstairs.

Lily stirred. Gone seven, the room was getting dark, the shadows making it harder to see. Turning on the desk lamp, she sat back, blinking in the sudden light. She'd only done about a third. As much as she typed, she deleted again, as if it were her fingers that were distracted rather than her mind running off in a tangent. Outside the window, the streetlights flickered once, then came on.

She reread what she'd written. It was okay, but nothing more. It lacked something. Conviction, maybe? She was writing something she didn't believe in, when normally she prided herself on her integrity. People might not agree with her opinion, or like her articles, but they couldn't fault her sincerity. Saving it, just in case, she opened a blank document. If she believed Ben's story was the crux of his work, how could she explore one without the other? But how could she explore a story she didn't believe, but had no real explanation for? Other than Ben was doing things without realising, or was lying, trying to manipulate her.

A gust of wind blew into the window, pressing at the glass and making the old panes rattle. Outside, the trees lining the street swayed, first one way and then the other, as the wind dropped and the limbs sprang back. Lily fancied more than heard the rustle of the leaves. Planted a century ago, they were London Plane, dark against the fading light, with thick, deeply ridged bark. Pruned, not once, or twice, but over and over. Whole limbs had been sawn off, leaving behind the scars of pale, raised whorls, as if they'd been hacked off in some ancient, bloody battle. It distorted the trunks, gave them the shape of a gothic nightmare, especially in the darkness. Up until now, she hadn't even let herself think of the face she'd seen in Highgate Wood. Dismissed as a trick of her hungover eye, could she really believe it was just another coincidence?

A line of cars passed down the street, their dipped lights flashing between the trees. The night changed everything. Turned the street into a dark, sinister place and filled the soft, tranquil forest and swathes of tall, high trees with supernatural creatures and wrinkled, child-eating witches. She stared at the blank page on the screen. She promised Ben she'd write the article, and she would keep her promise. But she couldn't leave it like that. She had to know what had happened, and why he'd drawn that picture of Anne Darrow dead, and why suffocation by leaves? Had to know, too, if what she'd seen was real, or just an elaborate con.

Doing it immediately, so she couldn't change her mind and back out, she went into her email and, writing a short message, sent it off to Veronica. She'd see it first thing tomorrow, and would either answer or simply call, whatever was easier for her. Ten minutes later, her mobile rang and, to Lily's surprise, it was her.

"Veronica! I wasn't expecting you to call."

"I saw your email."

"Yeah, but I meant for you to see it in the morning."

"Well, I've seen it, now," she replied testily. "So, tell me why you're looking for a police report on a woman who went missing years ago? And what this has to do with Ben Lewis?"

"Er, it's complicated."

"Then uncomplicate it."

Lily could almost see her face, the dark, impatient frown. She should've known that Veronica wouldn't just meekly accept her request. It was too out of character for someone like Lily to be looking into an artist's criminal background. It hinted at trouble, and Veronica hated trouble. If Lily wrote something that left the newspaper open to a defamation suit, it would be Veronica's neck on the line.

"I'm not quite sure what, but I know there's a story there. Something much bigger. And, er, I need a bit more information. For background."

Silence. Lily waited.

"Background?"

How did she get so much scorn into just one word?

"Look, Veronica, there isn't much. It's more gut feeling

than anything. It's just Ben has a drawing of her from two days before she disappeared. He met her in a park and he drew her. He was interviewed by the police and everything."

"So?"

"That's what I want. I believe Ben's work stems from that meeting and the realisation that he was one of the last people to see her. He was young, just fifteen, and it had a big impact."

"So, that's it?"

"I don't know." She didn't want to tell her about the second picture, and couldn't tell her about the face. Veronica would think she'd lost all sense, all reason. "I can't explain it. Let's just say my journalistic nose is twitching."

Veronica laughed. "Wine nose more like! From all those exhibitions. You're an art journalist and critic, Lily, not Kate Adie." She paused, thinking. "I suppose it could be interesting," she said eventually. "I remember Anne Darrow's disappearance was big, big news. There was something about her that really seemed to capture the public's imagination. I guess it was the way it happened. Hardly anyone seemed to know her, and those that did said she seemed a kind, lovely woman, but quiet. Lonely. And the police had no leads, no suspects, nothing. It was as if she'd vanished into thin air." Another pause. "But have you got his agreement?"

"No. At the moment, he doesn't want to talk about it."

"Then you don't have anything. We're not a tabloid, and your interviews rely on people wanting to talk to you. Break confidence and you'll lose your reputation, and no one will trust you, ever. And for what, a mildly interesting story?"

It sounded harsh, but Lily knew Veronica was just being realistic. But she also knew that if she could convince her, she'd back her all the way. Which was just one of the many reasons Lily preferred to work with her more than anyone else she knew.

"Obviously, what you do in your own time is up to you. I want your piece by next Friday at the latest. And whatever you're feeling, remember, I expect your usual standard."

"But that's the point – it can't be, because it won't be the artist's full story. It won't have the insight, the getting under the artist's skin, that is my raison d'etre."

"Then maybe you should try someone else. But do you have the time? I said I'd leave it up to you who you chose. But I want the five pieces on the city's up-and-coming artists I asked you to do on time."

She hadn't convinced her.

"Okay, then I'll stick with Ben," Lily agreed, giving up.

"But leave the police report with me. I'll talk with a colleague. Email me all the details."

"What? I don't understand?"

"Like you said, it's background. You could always do a follow-up, a second piece, as long as he agreed, of course."

They said their goodbyes. Although the conversation hadn't gone exactly how Lily had planned, she had what she wanted. Veronica obviously wasn't convinced, but had reasoned that she'd lose nothing by getting the information. She glanced at the clock. Just gone half seven. Meeting his brother, Anthony, Jeremy wouldn't be home until late. She should get something to eat. But after the conversation with Veronica, she was all fired up, determined to get the article finished. Food would have to wait. Opening the file she'd saved, she scrolled down to the last line and began to type.

*

It was almost eleven by the time Jeremy came in. She was in bed, ostensibly reading, although she hadn't even managed to reach the end of the chapter. Her head was too full of Ben and his story. If she considered just part of it, she could almost find some reason, but when you put it all together… his story, the drawings, the face…it just didn't make sense.

"Hi, darling!" Jeremy beamed, coming into the bedroom.

His face was flushed with the happy bonhomie of a few pints.

Lily lowered her book. "Good night?"

"Yeah, we couldn't decide where to eat, so went and got something at the pub." Closing the door, he came over to the bed.

"How is he?"

"Better. Better than I've seen him for a while."

Undoing his jeans, he pulled them down to his thighs before sitting down heavily on the bed, making the mattress bounce. Leaning forward, he pulled them the rest of the way, then, with an effort, started on his socks.

Fourteen months ago, Andrew's wife, Marjorie, had died of emphysema. She'd been a lifelong smoker, and had tried to give up so many times, but had always gone back. Anthony had cared for her right up until the end, and after her death, slowly, over about six months, his grief had turned into serious clinical depression. Jeremy had stayed with him for a few weeks, helping him to get support. He was much better now, although Lily wasn't sure he'd ever fully recover. Anthony was a few years older than Jeremy, and he and Marjorie had been together since they were teenagers. They had two kids, with families of their own, but both lived away, one in Carlisle, the other in America.

Lily had her lighter in her bag. Marjorie had had it for years; a chrome Zippo Anthony had bought for her, with her name engraved on a pearlized inset. The name Marjorie coming from the French for pearl. After her death, Anthony had thrown it out, but she'd retrieved it. She could understand his anger, but she'd seen Marjorie with it so many times it seemed almost part of her. So she slipped it into her bag, and left it there, as a way to keep Marjorie close. But over time, it had become almost a superstition, a talisman. Like a lock of hair in a locket, or a photograph. To carry a bag, and not have it in there, tucked in the very bottom, seemed odd, unnatural.

"How was your day?" Jeremy asked.

"Fine." She had thought of telling Jeremy about it, but the strangeness of it stopped her.

He'd been an accountant before he retired, concerned with the world of figures and facts, and although she knew he wouldn't laugh at her, she didn't think he'd agree with what she was doing either. Walk away, he'd say. What does it matter why Ben drew those pictures, or the story he told you? You've done your job. And as for the face; he's either lying, or if he believes what he says, he has a serious problem. Either way, it doesn't really have anything to do with you.

"So, is that it, you've finished?" he asked, taking off his shirt.

"Pretty much. There's just a couple of things."

Pulling back the duvet, he got into bed, the mattress bouncing again.

"Oh, right." He snuggled down beside her, yawning. "Are you staying reading?"

"No. I've got an appointment tomorrow morning, and have to leave early."

Putting the book down, she turned off the light and, rolling over, pressed her face in close. Almost immediately, a flush started, radiating out from the centre of her. For a moment, she waited, hoping it would pass, but when it didn't, she threw back the covers and moved away. Already fast asleep, Jeremy didn't even notice.

*

He was still asleep when she left the next morning, snoring gently. With a busy day ahead, and stuck, unable to do anything until she'd heard from Veronica, she pushed Ben and his story from her mind. There was something she could do, she realised, late that night, when she was almost asleep. More background. Wettin Park, the place where it had happened, was background. And going there, seeing it for herself, who knew what would come out of it? She was a visual person – it was part of her trade – and who knew, seeing the place for herself might give her a whole new perspective.

*

Thursday, and her first free morning, Lily caught the Tube and then the bus to Wettin Park. On her request, the driver shouted when the bus reached her stop, and with a quick thank you and wave, she bounced onto the pavement, feeling strangely invigorated. Was this how an investigative journalist felt on the scent of a story?

She'd lied to Jeremy. Told him she had another appointment and slipped on her trainers at the front door, so he didn't see. If he noticed she was wearing a pair of old jeans, and her rain jacket, he didn't say. She wanted to do this on her own, more to save her embarrassment than anything else.

With a high red brick wall to her left and a row of Victorian semis to her right, she followed the road, a long, squarish crescent, around to the entrance. Tall, Victorian iron gates, painted a flawless, glossy black, were just wide enough for a car, although a moveable bollard would stop anyone driving in who wasn't supposed to. Behind the gates, thick, dark green shrubbery reached up above the wall, hiding the park from view. Lily could be standing at the entrance to a stately home, a Victorian museum or even a cemetery.

She went through the gate, passed a mother with a pushchair and toddler, and followed the path through the two walls of green. Ahead, out the other side, a single Victorian iron lamppost stood on the side of the path, framed by open grass and a light blue sky. Thinking of Lucy, with her first glimpse of Narnia, she stepped out of the shrubbery.

A second path ran left and right, crossing the first like the bar of a 'T' and following the line of the wall. On the right bar sat a park bench and map, showing the layout of the park. Past the lamppost, the path curved upwards, toward the brow of the hill, with the rest of the park hidden out the other side. Except the wood. To the right of the path, it started just before the brow. Bunched tightly together, the trees, against the grass and the vast expense of the sky, reminded Lily of a single, thick tuft of hair on a smooth, shaven head. As if they didn't belong there. As if they'd been torn from a forest outside London, pulled up, roots and earth and all, and simply dropped there.

Crossing into the base of the 'T', Lily walked under the lamppost and towards the top of the hill. Coming the other way, the heads of a couple appeared. They reached the top and, stopping, turned to look at the view. Imagining it, out across London, it was tempting to join them. To ignore the worn grass track that moved off at a tangent towards the wood and continue along the path. But it wasn't why she was here, and besides, she could always come back that way. She stepped off the tarmac and onto the grass track.

It was colder out in the open. Fresh, bracing, the wind whipped around the trees, and sped across the grass, fuelled by the open space between the wood and the park's brick wall, like a tunnel. It caught her hair, blew it across her face and into her eyes, so that she had to hold it back.

She moved towards the wood, the trees growing steadily, like a plane coming into land. All broadleaf, some still had their leaves, their canopies turning from green to red, orange and yellow in a riot of colour. Others, including the sycamores, had already lost most of theirs. Almost there. Towering overhead, a line of sycamores loomed, their naked lower branches twisted sideways, as they reached out, towards the light. Beckoning, like arms. Come inside, Lily, come see.

Snaking between two hazel trees, their nuts gone, harvested and buried by the park's grey squirrels, the path disappeared into the centre of the wood. Reaching the entrance, she glanced back at the empty path and grass, and felt a sudden, inexplicable desire to turn around and flee. It was nothing; a touch of superstition, like Marjorie's lighter. Ignoring it, she followed the track into the wood, and the trees closed over her.

As with Highgate Wood, there was no carpet of leaves. Those that had fallen dotted the path, and here and there had gathered in small, deep patches; piles of green, yellow and red. Last year's fall lay half-mulched under the trees, its layers like an orgy of spring frogs, one on top of the other, inches deep.

She passed under more sycamores. Deeper, their fallen leaves already brown and curling, and she shuffled through the dusting, enjoying the sound as they crisped and crackled underfoot. She grinned, felt like a kid, as she kicked out first one foot and then the other, sending up small, half-hearted arcs that another time would be disappointing.

The sun winked at her through the trees as she continued through the wood, looking for the oak tree in Ben's drawing of Anne's body. Of course, it probably wasn't a real place, but what if it was? What if she found the actual place in his picture?

Between the branches were flashes of park, patches of neat, green grass, the tilt of the hill and the red brick wall. Full of the scents of autumn, it was bigger than it looked. Longer. It must take some work to look after it, but whoever did, they kept it immaculate. There wasn't a single piece of litter; not even a cigarette butt. There was no sign of the tree. And no strange atmosphere, no sense that anything bad had happened here. It was just a wood like any other. Travelling over, looking for something…some sense…she realised she could scan and search the ground, the undergrowth and the trees forever, but she'd never find anything, because there was nothing to find. She was chasing shadows. Making something out of nothing; a teenager's drawing that was in poor taste. He wouldn't be the first teenager to do that, or the last. At least Ben had some justification for it, with the trauma he'd suffered. And, as for the face…Lily, you're a fool, she told herself ruefully. Trying to be something you're not. You're an art critic, for Christ's sake. No wonder Veronica had scoffed.

Up until now, the path had been rising, but now it began to level out. It was hard to tell, but she thought she was coming to the centre. But with the trees all around her, metres deep, she could no longer see the park through the branches. And there was no one else in here; it was just her.

Ahead, slightly apart from the other trees, sat a huge oak tree. With its thick, gnarly trunk, it was another reminder of the magnificent forest that had once covered this part of the city. Ivy curled around its trunk, reached up high into the branches, as if reaching for the sky. Filling the gaps left between the trunk and the leaves, it puffed out the tree, cocooned its bark like a full-length body warmer. Stopping under it, she studied the rough, wrinkled bark and the shape of the branches.

That was it! The tree in Ben's picture. No, it wasn't, she thought, changing her mind. The shape wasn't quite right, although you could never be certain, with one oak tree surely looking like another. Inching closer, she reached out and pressed her hand on the trunk, and felt the rough, hard bark. It was surprisingly warm. For one fanciful moment, she thought she felt a throb of energy, coming from the ground into the roots and flowing up, up, through the trunk into the centre of the tree. A tree's heartbeat. Laughing inwardly at her silliness, she straightened just as, with a loud flurry of wings, a bird came crashing through the trees, sending leaves scattering and making her jump. Landing on a nearby willow, shining black, white and a deep, brilliant blue, as the thin branch dipped, it fixed its beady eye on her.

"Hello, Mr Magpie," Lily greeted him quietly.

But if he heard her, he showed no sign. A blink, a quick duck of his head and stretch of his wings and he was gone. Left alone, she turned the old rhyme over in my mind. *One for sorrow, two for joy…Seven for a secret never to be told.*

The wood darkened suddenly, as if the sun had gone behind a cloud. Almost immediately, the wind stirred, caressing her cheek, and she shivered. Just like it had the last day, in Highgate Wood with Jeremy, suddenly the trees seemed starker, the wood bleaker. Filled with grey, black and white; the colours of winter, as if, in the minutes she'd been in here, the seasons had turned again. Now this was the wood in Ben's story. The place where dark, supernatural faces stared malevolently out from the trees at you.

Another gust, and the leaves left on the trees rustled, and a branch creaked. It was time to go. Doing up the last button on her coat, the one tight to her neck, she stuffed her hands in her pockets and continued. There were no birds, no flutter of wings high above her head, as they flew from branch to branch.

The wind blew again, and the leaves on the ground behind her rustled, the sound long and sweeping, as if someone were dragging them along the ground. She glanced back, over one shoulder and, as the wind stopped, they shifted and settled.

She continued. Over the brow, the ground began to slope

downwards and around. Curling, as it wound around the hill, in the direction of the path. Unconsciously speeding up, letting the gradient take her, Lily passed silver birch, another oak and a horse chestnut, the first of the conker shells crunching underfoot like the bones of tiny animals. Another gust, and again it caught the leaves on the ground behind her, turning and shifting them like footsteps, and this time, when she looked, she stopped and turned. There was nothing there. Was this what Ben had seen? Anne letting her imagination, the human primeval fear of forests, overtake her?

Again, she continued, but hadn't gone more than three paces when the leaves rustled again. This time she ignored them. It couldn't be much further. Couldn't be long before she was stepping out from under the dark canopy and back into the open air, with people, and the rest of park beneath her, the busy city behind.

Behind her, the leaves weren't stopping, but were still moving, still rustling. The sound coming closer and closer, almost as if they were following her, stalking her. And then she realised there was no wind, and she whirled.

Leaves poured down the slope towards her like a shallow river. She looked left and right and saw more coming, slipping over patches of grass and through the weeds, as if pulled by magnets. They were coming up too. Defying gravity and pouring up the slope towards her. Streaming, coming from every angle, it was as if they were coming for her, as if she were the magnet. They reached her feet. Spilled onto her shoes and, with a cry, she jumped back. But they were still coming. Tumbling over one another, it was as if they were alive, a plague of beetles, scrambling and scratching, careless of everything in their eagerness to get to her. Too quick, her feet covered in seconds, as she watched, horrified, they began to pile in.

Past her ankles, the earth beneath her began to shift, the loose topsoil falling away, as if making room for her, and in a flash, she saw herself falling backwards, her feet sliding, unable to find purchase, and the leaves coming with her. She could almost feel them streaming up over her, along her arms and legs and across her chest. Heavy, pressing down, they would cover her body, until finally, helpless, unable to move, her head would fall back, and cold, wet leaves would slide across her cheeks and into her mouth and smother her. Something inside her broke. With another cry, she leapt up and out, her feet kicking, sending leaves scattering. It's not real! Spinning, she saw the leaves stop, as if waiting, and hearing a tree creak behind her, she spun again, following the sound.

Half-obscured, the face stared out at her from the leaves of a tree. Faintly green, its skin was rough and grained like bark, and its eyes rolled like marbles, with strands of green, brown-yellow, red and orange. Unblinking, they glared at her, the reds burning like tiny pieces of fire. Its lips pulled back and it was snarling, baring small, white-brown teeth. Lily flinched. She'd never seen such hatred. Unable to look away, she sensed more than saw the leaves begin again, slipping slowly towards her. Something was moving inside its mouth. She could see it through the gaps in the teeth; flashes of green, long and glistening wetly. And then, the mouth flexed, and very slowly, the teeth began to part.

"Lily! Lily! Lily!"

It was Jeremy's voice, echoing through the trees. He was

calling her, shouting her name over and over, the sound reaching up from the bottom of the wood. Even though she knew it couldn't be him, he wasn't there, it broke her stasis. Her breath coming out in a rush, she threw herself down the slope and began to run towards it, her feet slipping and sliding on the soft, rich earth. The wind was back, whipping down the path, making the trees around her shake. It was deafening, like the roar of an airplane, but still she heard Jeremy's voice, cutting through it like a beacon. The path rose over a steep hump and, panting, she pushed her legs up and over. She was almost there!

She could see the grass outside, a part of the park and the city behind it, between a break in the trees, like a tunnel, tantalisingly close. Something slithered past her feet, threatening to trip her, but desperation made her agile, and she danced away. Almost... almost...there. A final spurt of energy, a few more strides, then, she was out of the trees and onto the grass. The path was far to her left; she could see two figures sat on a park bench, and ran towards them. Halfway there her foot caught a tuft, and she fell, her body tipping forward and rolling.

Shocked, she lay still.

"Are you alright?" a voice called.

"Are you okay?"

The voice was coming closer, followed by the sound of someone running, and she began to struggle up.

"No, no, stay still," the voice said, its owner placing one hand on her shoulder.

She glimpsed a woman leaning, but it was all happening too quick. Ignoring her, she carried on, trying to pull herself up, but now there were more hands, trying awkwardly to hold her down.

"You shouldn't move. You might've hurt yerself," the woman urged.

"I'm – I'm okay," Lily replied, still struggling. "I want to get up."

"But you shouldn't," a second voice, another woman's, joined in. "At your age, falling like that, you could've done damage and not realise."

That did it.

"I'm fine, really. I want to get up." Breathing heavily, she pushed herself up, and reluctantly the hands fell away. "Really, I'm fine."

Straightening, she looked from one to the other. "Thank you. You're very kind, but I'm alright."

Both women, one was older. Lily guessed mid-forties, with light brown hair cut short. The other woman was much younger, her blonde hair tied back into a ponytail. She looked barely twenty, and was heavily pregnant. Mother and daughter, it had to be.

"You went down so hard. Are you sure you're alright?" the daughter asked. "You didn't hurt anything? Your ankle?"

"I don't think so." Lily took a few steps, checking it. "No, it seems fine. The only thing hurting is my pride. I feel like such an idiot."

"Well, you shouldn't. The ground is so wet. Only if you're sure," the older woman said doubtfully. "Maybe you should sit down for a minute and rest. There's a seat over there." She nodded towards the path.

"Yes, I think I will. Thanks."

Flanking her, as if they were afraid she might collapse, or run away, they walked with her to the seat.

"I didn't hurt you, did I, getting up like that?" she asked the young woman. "I didn't realise you were pregnant."

The young woman laughed. "No, I'm fine. And this one," she said, pointing to her stomach, "is going to be a right little bruiser, the way she kicks."

"Oh, you know it's a girl?"

"Yeah. Mum told us to wait. She said the surprise was nice, but I wanted to know."

She chatted all the way to the seat, telling Lily all about her baby, her mum chipping in every so often. At the seat, they watched her sit, then hovered, still chatting.

"Are you sure you're okay?" the mother asked again.

"Yes, thank you." Lily gave them her best smile. "But thank you so much for your help."

They beamed.

"We should go," the mother said to her daughter. "You need to get home and rest."

Lily moved along the bench. "Do you want to sit down? There's plenty of room."

"No. I'm fine. We take it slow; don't we, mum? And its downhill all the way."

Thanking them again, Lily watched as they walked slowly down the hill. Alone again, suddenly, she wished they were staying. Their bright, busy chat made everything normal. But things were anything but normal. From here, the wood looked hunched, like an animal clinging to the side of the hill, its belly low to the ground. Hiding, or maybe, guarding its secret. She shuddered, remembering the feel of the leaves across her feet and her ankles, pressing down even as the soil beneath her gave way. As if they were working together, trying to make her disappear. Like Anne Darrow. That could have been her, lying on her back, her eyes open and her mouth full of leaves. Stop it, Lily, she told herself quickly. It's not real.

She was so cold, and felt sick, almost fluey. It's the shock, a voice inside her said, dispassionate. You need tea, or a stiff drink.

She closed her eyes. She didn't want to believe it, but she had no choice. Ben's face was real. Everything he'd told her was real. She opened her eyes. Except he hadn't told her that he'd seen Anne dead. Hadn't told the police either. But why? Because they would never have believed him, that's why. They'd've sent him to a psychiatrist, or worse. But how could he have just left her like that? And where was her body? She thought of the movement of the soil, the feeling that it was falling in, preparing to take her with it. The wood had buried it. And, maybe, in the horror of it, Ben had just run. Finding the body like that, he was only a kid, and he'd've seen the face on his picture by then. Or maybe, it had still been there, watching, waiting for the earth to slowly devour her body.

She had to tell him. Had to explain that she knew now, and understood. Taking out her phone, she scrolled to his number with shaking fingers and called his number. It rang a few times, then switched to voicemail, and she hung up. Then, after a moment's thought, she called him back.

"Ben, it's Lily. Can you call me as soon as you get this? It's important. Thanks."

Hanging up for a second time, she slipped the phone back in her bag. Maybe she should go straight to his studio. He was probably there, working. It wasn't far; she could get a taxi. Pressing both hands to the seat, she pulled herself up and, for the first time, noticed the mud down one leg and on one side of her coat. Maybe not. Seeing her like that might freak him out. And he might not even be there. She didn't think she could bear a wasted journey; not after that. She should go home and change, and maybe think about what exactly she was going to say to him.

She couldn't face walking up, past the wood, even though it wasn't that close, so she went downwards, following the two women.

Chapter Five

In the end, getting money out of a cashpoint, she caught a taxi home. Luckily, the driver's English wasn't too good, so he didn't talk much. And if he noticed the mud, he either didn't have the words to ask or felt it was none of his business.

Sat in the back, gazing at London life rolling by through a thin pane of glass, that might well have been the light years of space, she'd never felt so utterly alone before. Was this how Ben had felt? As if he were lost and alone on the dark and empty moon, looking down at the green and blue earth? No wonder he'd tried to bury it.

Jeremy was in his room at the top of the house. A typical accountant, he'd invested most of his inheritance from the sale of the family home, but she'd managed to persuade him to keep some back for a loft conversion. Now the whole space was his, to do exactly what he wanted with. Except, when her sisters came with the kids, and the kids took it as a bedroom and playroom, but that wasn't often. Almost grown, they hadn't stayed for a couple of years.

It was easy to sneak into the bedroom and change her jeans. Placing the dirty ones in the linen basket in the bathroom, she caught sight of herself in the mirror. Her face looked the same as usual, normal, as if nothing out of the ordinary had happened. As if the world was still the same place it had been a few hours ago.

"Do you want a drink? I'm making one," she shouted up the narrow, second stairs.

The urge to go up there and see him, to put her arms around him and pull him close, was almost overwhelming, but she resisted. He'd only want to know what was wrong, and she couldn't bear to tell him, and see that look on his face. The look Ben had probably seen on hers.

"Oh, you're back. No, thanks, I'm fine."

"Okay, then."

Pouring herself a whiskey, she took a gulp, feeling the liquid warm her all the way down. That was better. She took it upstairs, into her office. Ben still hadn't replied. Of course, he could be busy, but she thought, more likely, he was avoiding her. And who could blame him?

She took a sip then, placing the glass and her phone on the desk next to her, she turned on her laptop and waited for it to load. She and Ben couldn't be the only ones to have seen the face. Someone, somewhere, must have seen it too. The laptop loaded, and she tapped in her password. She called it a Green Man, but she didn't really know what it was. She hadn't seen its body, whatever it looked like; it had been obscured by the vegetation. All she'd seen was a face in the leaves. The Green Man; it seemed the best place to start.

Another sip, and she began to search, but there was an awful lot of fiction parading as fact, and no one seemed to know where it came from, although there were a few theories.

The name had been coined in Britain by a Lady Raglan in nineteen thirty-nine, and although images of the Green Man seemed to be concentrated in Britain and France, they were found across Europe.

She began to pore through photographs. Carved and etched into stone, wood and metal, throughout the centuries, the Green Man was found in church roofs, entrances and the tops of columns, gazing down at parishioners, smiling, scowling and grimacing. Some peered out of leaves, others spewed out of vegetation; vines, leaves and branches. The Green Man was in Canterbury Cathedral, York Minster and churches from Staffordshire to Hertfordshire, Yorkshire to Devon. He was in Normandy, the Dordogne and Roman Germany, Italy and even part of a Roman mosaic in Istanbul. He was in first-century, Mesopotamia, Hatra in Iraq, eighth-century Rajasthan, India and even Benin in Africa.

Her whiskey untouched, wrapped up in her search, she didn't even notice. Born of the forest, of its rich, verdant green, to some, the Green Man was Puck, or Robin Goodfellow, Shakespeare's mischievous wood sprite. Or Robin Hood, Herne the Hunter or even the Green Knight from King Arthur. As if these legends were rooted in an older, more primitive belief. Like the Roman God of the forest, Silvanus, or the Celtic deity, Cernunnos.

But maybe, Lily thought, resting her chin on her hand, as she scrolled through a second website filled with yet more pictures, the Green Man was in all of them, just given a different name, a different face, depending on the people, their culture and their religions. Maybe he was there right from the beginning, with the first humans, deep in the forests of Africa, protecting the forest and holding the humans that used it to account.

She clicked on another photo, this one from Rosslyn Chapel in Scotland, the face small, round, like a toddler, or a cherub, with a thin vine across its mouth.

It was all conjecture. Guesswork, making connections that may or may not be there, interpreting the past through modern eyes. Nothing looked like what she'd seen, or what had happened. Although, now she thought about it, what exactly had happened? The wind had blown leaves over her feet, and she thought she'd seen a face in the trees. And as for Anne Darrow, maybe nothing had happened to her, and she'd simply wanted to disappear, for her own reasons.

She rubbed her eyes. She was like a dog chasing its tail, going round and round in circles. As if, even after everything, part of her refused to believe what she saw. Another click, and a new photo appeared. That was it! That was the face, or pretty close to it. She leant forward. On second thoughts, it wasn't that close, but it was enough of a likeness to send a shiver up her spine. Found in Rochester Cathedral in Kent, it was carved in wood and then painted, brown and green. Like the face in Rosslyn Chapel, it had a vine, or was it a branch, between its teeth, stretched across like a gag. No, that wasn't right. There were two branches, not one, coming from inside the mouth, gorging, spewing outwards. As if it were creating, giving birth, to the forest.

Sitting back, she stared at the photo. There was no anger in this face, no hatred, or deep, dark malice; it was expressionless. Was that due to the carver's level of skill, or something else? If you were Silvanus or Cernunnos, and saw your world being destroyed, over and over, then shrunk almost to nothing… maybe that fury had come later.

She clicked again. Found in Shebbear, Devon, and etched in metal, a skull grimaced, showing its teeth, while sprouted vines or tendrils grew out its empty eye sockets. She thought of the shifting soil beneath her feet, and the feeling that she was going to fall and the leaves and earth would cover her. Was this a Green Man, or one of its victims? How many people had vanished down the centuries? It couldn't be all of them, but a few, perhaps? One or two a year… so many people went missing, never to be found, who'd know?

She looked at her phone. Ben wasn't going to reply; she was going to have to call again. Picking it up, she scrolled to his number and pressed call.

"Ben, it's Lily, again. Please call me as soon as you can. It really is important. Thanks."

She hung up. Placed her phone down on the desk, and immediately it began to ring. Snatching it up, she answered it without checking the number.

"Hello, Ben!"

"Lily? No, it's Mark, Mark Langley. Veronica asked me to call. About Ben Lewis."

She'd met him a couple of times, but briefly; he worked largely in crime reporting.

"Oh, great. Thanks, Mark."

"Don't thank me yet. I'll email over what I have. The interview with Ben Lewis seems pretty standard. He was one of about ten eye witnesses."

"What do they think happened to Anne Darrow?"

"Other than they think she's probably dead? Their

investigation was inconclusive, obviously. A few people had seen her on that last day; the last witness saw her around half three, then nothing. But there was no indication that she'd gone anywhere. Her flat looked as if she'd just gone out for a time, with no plans not to return. But it was before there were cameras everywhere. She literally seemed to disappear."

"Okay, but thanks anyway." It was hard to keep the disappointment out of her voice.

"But there's something else. This wasn't the only time Ben Lewis helped the police."

"Oh?"

"When he was seven, he came across a body in the woods."

"What?!"

"In Epping Forest. He was playing there, in the part called Great Monk's Wood, with his older brother and some friends, and he'd wandered off alone. The family lived in Loughton for a while – needlessly to say, they moved after that. It was a young woman. Her name was Sally Longmate. She was asphyxiated, murdered."

"How?" Lily heard herself whisper.

"Her mouth was full of leaves. Someone used them to smother her."

Lily's throat stuck. She swallowed, trying to lubricate it. "D— did they catch him?"

"No. There was no evidence, no DNA, no nothing. There was a boyfriend, but he was away working. He was plasterer, and his firm was renovating some big hotel in Devon. Of course, they checked it all out. They didn't release Ben's name at the time, for his own protection, more from the tabloid press than anything else. I would imagine, even then, they'd have got a psychologist involved for the poor kid." He paused. "Veronica didn't say why you were so interested, but this isn't your usual area, is it?"

He was fishing. A missing person was one thing, but an unsolved grisly murder quite another.

"Oh, it's just background for a piece I'm doing. It explores how a trauma in childhood influences the creative genius. I hope I haven't disappointed you."

"No, it sounds interesting," he lied. "Well, let me know, if you need any more help."

"Yeah, I will. Thanks, Mark. I really appreciate it. Er, there's a new exhibition on at the Barbican. The tickets are quite sought after, but I could get you a couple, if you're interested. As a way of saying thanks. It's modern, explorative art, using dance and dolphin sounds played through giant speakers, I'm sure you'd like it."

"No, you're alright," he said quickly. "But thanks, I appreciate the thought."

She stifled a laugh. "That's a shame. But thanks again, Mark. Bye, bye."

He hung up. Hopefully that had done the trick, and he'd avoid her from now on. Unless, of course, he checked the list of events at the Barbican and realised there was no such exhibition, but she doubted he'd think her so duplicitous. She wasn't a real journalist, after all.

Still holding her phone, she looked down at her scribbled notes. It was all starting to make a weird, horrible sense. Like pieces of a puzzle slotting into a place that you think can't possibly be right, but when you finish, and you see the whole picture, you realise it must be. She needed to speak to Ben, as much for herself now as for him. She looked at her watch. Five past two. He'd told her he volunteered at the local school Thursday afternoons, so there was no way he'd reply now. It was just one of the many reasons she liked him.

"Hi." Jeremy's head appeared around the door. "Have you had lunch yet?"

"No, not yet." She shook her head.

"Then down in ten minutes. Whatever you're doing, it'll keep." His head disappeared.

*

Ben didn't call back later; not that evening, or that night. She tried him again, first thing the next morning, and left another message. And then again, at half twelve, hoping she'd get him on a break, and this time, to her surprise, he answered.

"Why do you keep ringing me?"

"Ben, I have to tell you something." Lily stopped – now that she was finally talking to him, she wasn't sure where to begin.

"Have you heard from yer editor?"

"No, not yet."

"Then I don't wanna know. I've been thinking, and I don't want to talk to you anymore."

"But I've found out something important. Look, I can't talk on the phone, can we meet somewhere? The studio, or somewhere else? Whatever you prefer."

There was a pause.

"No, I told you, I'm not interested," he replied. "Look, I just want to draw. I don't care about anything else. I don't care what happened. It's gone, over with."

"But it's not. It's still there in your pictures. Don't you want to know–?"

"No, I don't. I told you, I don't want to hear about it. Just go away and leave me alone. If I knew it would be like this, I'd never have done the fucking interview!"

"I'm sorry I didn't believe you, but—"

"Why don't you listen?!" His voice throbbed with anger, but somehow, he controlled it. "I told you, I don't care. I've got to go."

"Wait, don't hang up, please, Ben," she said desperately. "I went to Wettin Park, to the woods, and I saw it. I saw the face."

He didn't answer, but he didn't hang up either.

"I saw it. I know it's real." Still no answer. "Ben, Ben? Are you listening?"

"Yeah."

"I'm so sorry I doubted you. I know now it's true. It's all true."

"What do you want me to say?" he demanded, his voice sullen. "It doesn't change anything. How many times do I have to tell you, I don't care?"

"But you do, I know you do. I can't imagine what it's been like all these years, not daring to tell anyone, because you're afraid they wouldn't believe you, and then, finally you tell someone, you tell me, and I didn't believe you, and I'm so sorry." She stopped, pausing for breath, then continued. "But, Ben, there's something else. I know I shouldn't've done it, but while you were, er, making the drinks, I, er, looked in the second envelope. I saw the drawing you did."

"What?! You're unbelievable!"

He began to swear. He was going to hang up, she was sure of it.

"Please, Ben, don't hang up. I know who she is, and I found out—"

"I know who she sodding is! She's Anne Darrow."

"Anne Darrow?! Oh, no, I thought you knew. It's not her, it's—"

"It was horrible," he continued, not listening. "I was having nightmares. I kept seeing her like that, over and over. It seemed so real. Like I was actually there. I don't why I drew it, it was like, I just had to get it out of my head before I lost my mind. And it worked, but after seeing it, it kinda scared me. I mean, I never saw her like that, I swear. So, I put it away, and I haven't looked at it since."

"Why didn't you destroy it?"

"I dunno. I was afraid, I guess."

In case the nightmares came back. She'd've probably done the same.

"Wait a minute, you said it wasn't Anne Darrow," he said, realising finally. "What do you mean?"

"Ben, I really think I should tell you face to face rather than over the phone. I can come to you now if you like."

"No. I want you tell me, right now, or that's it. Who is she?"

Lily sighed. It was too late to back out now. If she'd realised that he didn't remember, she'd never had said it over the phone. "I promise you, I really thought you knew. The woman in your drawing is a woman called Sally Longmate."

"Sally Longmate, who's she?"

"She was murdered in Epping Forest. Her body found by a seven-year-old boy. The family lived in Loughton and he was playing in the woods with his older brother and his friends. He found her, just as she was in your picture." She paused. "Ben, that little boy was you."

"Me?! No, it couldn't be. I'd know, I'd remember."

"Not necessarily. It's not uncommon for young kids to forget traumatic events. They're too young, they can't cope, can't deal with what they've seen, so they just forget. And your parents moving probably helped that."

Silence.

"Say something, Ben."

"We used to live in Loughton. I remember the woods too."

"But nothing about that day?"

"No." She could hear the confusion in his voice, the doubt. "I need to think."

"You need to take it easy. It'll probably take some time to get your head—"

"Two of 'em. Why two of 'em?" he cried, his accent becoming broader, more pronounced in his distress. "And why me? Why did I see them? Why not someone else? And why is the face in my pictures?"

"I see it too; you're not the only one."

But he had a point. Why did they see it, and not anyone else?

"Gotta go," he said abruptly.

"Ben, wait, you—"

But it was too late, he'd hung up.

Immediately, she called him back, but his phone went to voicemail, so she hung up and tried again. This time a mechanised voice told her the number was unavailable. He'd switched it off.

"Shit!"

She wanted to go over there, but she knew she shouldn't. He wasn't a child, he was a grown man, and besides, he needed time to calm down. But it sounded as if he were blaming himself. What if he did something stupid?

She didn't know how long she sat there, staring into space, thinking. Jeremy was in the garden, cutting back the dead flowers, but he looked up when she opened the kitchen door and joined him outside.

"Everything alright?"

"No, not really."

How did he always know when something wasn't right?

*

Sat together at the kitchen table, she told him everything, leaving nothing out. She kept waiting for him to say something, to make a comment, or ask a question, but he didn't.

When she'd finished, he got to his feet.

"Fancy a tea?" he asked, going over to the kettle.

She didn't quite know what to say. "Yeah, okay, thanks."

She watched him make the drinks. He didn't believe her. Of course he didn't believe her. How could anyone believe her?

"There you go."

He placed the mug down in front of her, next to her phone, then returned to his seat.

"Jeremy, for God's sake, say something!"

He looked straight into her eyes. "What do you want me to say?"

"I dunno, something, anything. That you believe me."

He flopped back with a sigh. "How can I believe you?"

Her heart sank. Knowing something and hearing it were two different things.

"And yet, I do. I'll always believe you, Lily. I can't help it, I love you, so I'll always believe you, no matter what you say, even if it is impossible."

"Oh, Jeremy!" Something broke inside her. Tears welling, she leapt to her feet and threw her arms around him.

"Why didn't you tell me?" he asked as she let him go. "I knew something was wrong; you've been so distracted the last week. I began to think you were seeing someone."

That made her laugh. Wiping at her eyes, she was trying to think of a smart answer when her phone rang. Diving for it, she glanced at the number as she answered it, but it wasn't one she recognised.

"Hello, Lily Goodfellow," she said shakily.

"Miss Goodfellow, its Amelia."

It took her a minute. "Amelia? Oh, yes, hi Amelia."

"I don't know if this is okay, but I didn't know who else to call," she said breathlessly, talking fast. "I got your number from the book in reception. It's Ben."

"Is he alright?"

"No, he's really bad. I went to the studio to see him and he was shouting, raving. He kept talking about you." Her voice broke, and she began to sob. "He'd destroyed all his pictures. He said they were bad, infected, and he slashed them with a knife. They're…ruined!"

"Shit!" She glanced at Jeremy. "Amelia, where is he now?"

Still sobbing, she didn't answer.

"Amelia?!"

Gulping, she tried to gain control of herself. "He's… gone… to Epping Forest."

"Epping Forest?! Did he say why?"

She sniffed loudly. "He just kept saying that he needed answers. I wanted to go with him, but he wouldn't let me. He made me promise not to tell his parents, and I didn't know what to do."

"When did he leave?"

Another sniff. "I dunno. About half an hour ago."

"Half an hour," Lily repeated, for Jeremy's sake. "Okay, okay. Amelia, you did the right thing."

Grabbing the car keys off the side, Jeremy held them up and Lily nodded.

"I think I should tell his mum," Amelia was saying.

"Maybe leave it a while. We're going over there to see if we can find him. This is my fault. I need to see him and explain, and we don't want to worry her for nothing, do we?"

"I suppose." She swallowed noisily. "You don't think… he'll do something, do you?"

"No, of course not. Did he tell you what happened in Epping?"

"No. Like I said, he was talking about you. He said that after what you'd told him, he'd started to remember, from when he was a kid. Something bad. I asked him, but he wouldn't tell me. And then, when he said he was going, I said I'd come too. I didn't mean anything, I just wanted to help him, but he shouted at me. I was so scared. I've never heard him shout like that before."

"I'm sure he didn't mean it. I think he was just stressed. And you are helping him, Amelia, by calling me. You did exactly the right thing. Look, give me his mum's number, so I can call her if I need to."

"I'll text it to you, it'll be quicker."

"Great, thanks. We're leaving now."

"Will you call me? Let me know when you've found him?"

"Of course I will," Lily said soothingly. "Try not to worry, I'm sure he's fine."

"Okay… Bye then."

"Bye."

Hanging up, she looked at Jeremy. "We need to go. This is all my fault. If I hadn't interfered, he never would have remembered and gone back to Epping."

"I'll get my shoes." Moving past her, he disappeared into the hall.

She went to follow him, but on impulse, thinking that it might help if they got caught in the forest in the dark, she grabbed her handbag off the table and, reaching in, pulled out Marjorie's lighter.

"Ready?" he asked from the doorway.

"Yep," she replied, quickly stuffing it into her back pocket.

Outside, key in the ignition, he started the car.

"Where to do I head for? Epping's a big place," he asked, lifting the handbrake.

"Just head towards it. I know where it happened; it's called Great Monk's Wood. I just need find the directions." She took out her phone. "I'll look it up while you drive."

Chapter Six

They didn't talk much on the way over, just about the directions. Lily thought Jeremy must have so many questions, although she didn't think she could answer them, but now was not the time. If Ben saw the Green Man in Epping Forest, she dreaded to think what would happen to him.

Jeremy found a space on the busy residential road, about fifty metres from the entrance. Getting out, he locked the car and they looked around them.

"Miss Goodfellow, Lily?!"

Realising someone was calling her, Lily turned, Jeremy a second behind her. Wearing an electric blue short puffer jacket and skinny jeans, Amelia appeared from behind a high white van parked the other side of the road, her arm raised.

"Lily!" She waved her hand frantically. "Wait!"

A glance right and left, and then weaving expertly between the traffic, she dashed across the road.

"Amelia! What are you doing here?!" Lily demanded as she reached them.

"I'm sorry, but I had to come. I couldn't just sit and wait. He is my boyfriend."

"Yes, I know, but it's—" She stopped. She was going to say it wasn't safe, but that would only lead to difficult questions. "You should go. Ben didn't want you here."

"I don't care. I have to know he's okay." Amelia stuck out her chin. "You can't stop me. I'm not a child."

Helpless, Lily looked at Jeremy.

"She's right, we can't stop her. And maybe it would be better if she were with us?"

He had a point. She'd just follow them anyway, or worse, go off alone. At least this way they would be all together. She was certain that if anything were to happen, it would be when one of them were left on their own.

"Alright. But only if you stay with us, and don't go wandering off. It's not – it's important, really important, we all stick together. Do you promise?"

She made her sound about six. For a moment, she thought Amelia was going to refuse, but then she nodded. "Okay."

"Right. Let's go."

Walking fast, they reached the entrance. Stepping inside, under the trees, Lily paused. Five paths led into the forest, like the spokes of the wheel. Leaves dotted the paths, bunched at the edges, but she refused to look at them.

"Hmm." It was hard to be certain. Now she was here, it all looked the same. "I think it's that way," she said eventually, pointing to the second right.

"You think?!" Amelia exclaimed loudly; her cheeks flushing a fiery, angry red. "I thought you knew!"

Reaching into her coat pocket, she took out her phone and, holding it in one hand, using her thumb and fingers, began tapping furiously.

"I know the place," Lily found herself explaining. "But I had to look up the directions up in the car, and—"

"It's okay, I've got it. I tracked his phone."

"You tracked his phone? Is that legal?"

"Who cares?!" she snorted. "If it finds him."

"Why didn't you say?"

"Like I said, I thought you knew where you were going, but apparently not."

There was a pause. Waiting, Lily looked at Jeremy, but he was staring at Amelia, his face unreadable.

"Got him," she announced, after what seemed like forever. "That way." Holding her phone out in front her of, she shot away, down the second right path.

"Just like I said," Lily complained, following.

Overgrown, the tips of the branches leaning and brushing their arms and shoulders, like a cavalcade of ardent fans, the path meandered. In front, Amelia was charging ahead.

"Amelia, slow down!" Jeremy called. "We have to stay together."

No answer. With a spurt of energy, he moved in front of Lily, his arms swinging. She tried to match his speed, but with his long legs and daily walks, he was just too fast. Not wanting to be left behind, she pushed her legs harder.

Minutes passed. With the distance between them, Jeremy was the bridge, the go-between, the only one keeping them both in sight. Around them, the forest looked all the same, with the same trees, the same undergrowth, not that there was time to look too closely, and the path endless. Lily lost count of the twists and turns. Another corner, and ahead, Amelia had reached a crossroads. She didn't hesitate, but tore straight across. Thank God for her phone and her dodgy tracker, Lily thought; they'd never have found Ben without it.

They continued, going deeper into the forest. Overhead, the late afternoon sky was dull and grey. They had about two hours of light left. Or with the thick, heavy cloud, maybe less. They needed to find Ben and get out. There was no way she wanted to be in here in the dark.

Breathing heavily, Lily turned another corner and the path straightened out before her. Halfway along, Amelia had stopped and was peering into the overgrowth.

"Come on!" she shouted, seeing them coming. "It's not far. We're almost there."

"Wait for Lily," Jeremy called back.

He'd almost reached her. Ignoring the protest in her legs, Lily sped up. It was the wine, and the rich, delicious hors d'oevres at opening nights. Just one more. Well, no more. After this, she'd make sure she went out walking with Jeremy. No excuses.

"Hurry up!" Amelia shifted from foot to foot. It was only Jeremy that was stopping her from plunging headfirst into the green.

Reaching them finally, now Lily could see the gap in the trees, and the track that led even deeper into the forest.

"Let's go," Amelia said.

"Just…one…minute," Lily breathed, bending forward. It felt good to stop, if only for a moment.

"Are you alright?" Jeremy asked, touching her shoulder.

"Yeah…fine." She straightened. "Too unfit."

"We don't have time for this. We have to go!" Amelia all but stamped her foot in her impatience.

"I'm ready."

It was all Amelia needed. Throwing herself onto the track,

she disappeared into the trees. Without a word, Jeremy went after her, Lily following.

The track was just wide enough for one person. Lily pushed her way through the overhanging branches. Wet from the recent rain, water dropped onto her arms and shoulders and slowly soaked her through. The same rain made underfoot treacherous, the wet fallen leaves and exposed tree roots slippery like ice. Jeremy was just ahead of her. She heard him swear as his foot skidded in the soft, loose soil, pushing and pressing it up into a small ridge of mud.

"Shit!" he swore, righting himself before looking back. "Lily, I'm losing her."

"Then go."

"I'm not leaving you."

"You're not. I'm right behind you. But you can't lose her. This is all my fault. We can't let anything happen to her."

Reluctant, flashing her a dubious look, he sped up, his feet slipping. It was all her fault – if only she hadn't been so nosey, and opened Ben's portfolio, like Pandora and her bloody box.

They continued. The track seemed to go on forever, twisting around trees and patches of weeds, although it couldn't be much more than five, maybe ten minutes. Alone more and more, with just the occasional glimpse of Jeremy's back as he turned a corner ahead of her, she could follow him by the sound, the rustle and swoosh as he pushed his body through the branches.

Her foot caught a tree root and, tripping forward, she would've fallen if it hadn't been for a quick grab of a branch. Small, the thin wood bending and dipping, for a moment she swayed precariously. She looked down and saw the leaves and shuddered. The thought of landing on top of them, and feeling them moving and slipping beneath her, was too much. Even now, she could imagine them sliding towards her, their rustle slow and deep as they came for her. She let go of the branch. She couldn't let herself think about it. She had to keep moving, had to get to Ben. If anything happened to him in here… gritting her teeth, she continued.

She'd wasted precious minutes, and couldn't see Jeremy at all now, although she could still hear him. It couldn't be much further, surely? Amelia had said Ben was close, only it didn't seem it. It seemed as if they'd been on this track, pushing through the trees, for hours.

"Amelia! Amelia!" It was Jeremy. He was shouting, his voice echoing through the trees and up into the treetops.

Lily went cold. Oh, God, had he lost her?!

"Amelia! Amelia!"

Jeremy's shout galvanised her. She flew around the next corner, straight into a line of trees. Skidding to a stop, she stared at them in surprise. It was a dead end. The path just stopped.

Confused, she peered into the gloom, thinking that maybe the trees had grown into it, and it started again, out the other side, but there was no sign of a path. No break, or gaps in the trees, for as far as she could see. Just dark, endless vegetation. But trees couldn't just spring up like that, barring her way. The path, and Jeremy and Amelia, had to be somewhere nearby.

"Jeremy!" she shouted. "Amelia!"

Spinning, she looked about her. To her left, a trail of flattened grass moved away at right angles.

"Lily?! Where are you?"

Jeremy's voice seemed to come from all directions. She

couldn't pinpoint it. But there was nowhere else to go; they had to have gone left. She dashed down the trail, following them.

Ploughing through ferns, their leaves swishing softly against her jeans, she watched the ground carefully, making sure she didn't go wrong. Following their tracks, as they weaved through the trees, she had no real idea of where she was going, or if this would lead back to the track, or maybe another path altogether. There was no straight line, no rationale why their tracks bent one way and not the other, but she guessed Jeremy was just following Amelia, and she was following her phone.

"Jeremy! Jeremy!" she shouted, ducking under a low hanging branch.

No answer. He must be able to hear her; he couldn't have gone that far. It was as if the trees were a wall, or the shifting sands of the desert, deliberately keeping them apart. Her heart began to pound. What if she was stuck in here, all alone, until darkness descended? And the others too. She didn't want to think what could happen to them. How the forest could make them disappear, like Anne Darrow and Sally Longmate. She had to find them and get out of here.

She stopped and, bending over with the effort, screamed as loud as she could, like a child.

"Jeremy! Where are you? Jeremy!" Her voice cracked, her breath catching the back of her throat.

Still no answer. She listened, fighting the urge to cough, her ears straining.

"Lily?" It was faint, coming from somewhere ahead.

"I'm coming, Jeremy. Wait for me."

She had to cough, small, short hacks, as she moved towards

his voice.

"Lily? Lily?"

The forest was changing, becoming thicker, denser. Small, thin trees crowded in on one another, even the small space between them overtaken by thin, scraggy bush. Above, the sky was beginning to darken, sending shadows.

"Lily?"

She was getting closer, his voice getting louder. She'd lost their trail, couldn't see where their feet had been, but it couldn't be much further. There was no time to wonder where Amelia was, or how close they were to Ben. A fallen tree lay across her way, like the carcase of a dead animal. Its trunk narrow, there was no need to go around it, so she stepped awkwardly over the top, broken off, half-rotten branches snapping loudly beneath her feet. Overhead, the trees swayed in a sudden gust of wind, those still with leaves rustling, and she caught the scent of crumbling, decaying wood.

"Lily," Jeremy called again, his voice merging with the wind and the trees, so that it seemed almost part of their murmur.

The back of her neck pricked. Like a dog lifting its head and sniffing cautiously, but desperate to reach him, she ignored it.

"I'm coming."

Pushing through a thick line of trees and bush, bending the branches back with her hands and her wrists, just enough to squeeze past, she slowed to a crawl. Despite the noise she was making, she heard a sound, coming from somewhere to her right, like someone shuffling through the undergrowth. She turned and saw the leaves on a thicket of hawthorns stir. Jeremy! Thank God. As she took a step towards him, the leaves parted, and a face appeared, staring out of the green at her.

Her stomach dropped. It was the Green Man; its multicoloured eyes, like marbles, glaring. Pale green skin glistened; as if, like the rest of the forest, it was still damp from the rain. Its mouth closed, even as she stared, frozen, mesmerised with horror, and the lips opened, revealing short, white-brown teeth. Behind them, something was moving, slipping past the gaps between the teeth, like a shadow. She heard a creak, and a soft, wet rasp, and then the teeth parted and the lips split into a wide, vicious grin. Long, thin, it was a vine, or a tendril, its pale green surface glistening, as if covered with slime. And it was turning, sliding inside the mouth, around and around, as if it were a circle coming back on itself in a loop. Another creak, and soft white spittle formed along its edges, then dropped onto the teeth, smearing the lips and the side of the mouth. Only it wasn't spittle – it was sap. Her hand flying to her mouth, she took a step back, and then she heard it; the rustle of leaves.

Whirling, her feet seeming to move by themselves, she charged headfirst through the trees and vegetation, using her arms and shoulders to push her way through. Branches scratched at her body, her head, snagging her hair like hooked fingers. One snapped back and, swinging low and wide, caught her across the face, stinging her skin like a whip. Her breath gasping, her heart pounding, she couldn't stop, couldn't slow. She had to get out, to get away.

Her foot caught a bramble. One moment she was upright, and the next she was bouncing and rolling though the ferns. Unharmed, she staggered up, but she'd lost her bearings and didn't know which way to go.

"Jeremy!" she screamed.

No answer. She couldn't wait; she had to move. She threw herself forward.

Ahead, a late patch of stinging nettles rose high above her head. Turning sharply, she veered around it and almost staggered straight into a holly bush. Panting, she veered again, left this time and, turning sideways, slipped in between the holly and a line of hazel. Holly leaves pricked her shoulders and back, and then she was stepping, almost falling out, onto the track beyond. She'd done it! Almost sobbing with relief, her chest heaving and her legs like lead, she bent forward, trying to catch her breath.

Looking down, it took her a moment to realise what she was standing on. A carpet of brown leaves, an inch deep. Her breath caught, and she straightened. They were everywhere. This wasn't the path. It was the wide, open ground of another part of the forest. Here, the ground was sweeping and undulating, the trees huge, centuries old, sycamore, beech, ash and oak, their trunks heavy, misshapen, with vast, empty canopies. The only way was back.

Slowly, carefully, she took a step back, wincing as the leaves underfoot crunched. Something moved in the bushes behind her, and this time, she didn't have to look; she knew exactly what it was.

To her left, a few leaves lifted and turned over, as if caught by a breeze. More turned, then tumbled backwards, as those beneath shifted forward in one long drag that sounded like a body being pulled along the ground. And then the leaves around her feet began to move, to brush against her shoes like water lapping and, with a loud, echoing cry, she turned right and ran.

Her leaden legs pumping, she ran with a strength she didn't know she had. The leaves were shifting beneath her, rippling and undulating like a restless tide. It was hard to keep her footing, but she knew what would happen if she fell. Instinctively searching for higher ground, she danced across them, leaping from tree root to tree root. But she was tiring, with the start of a stitch. Pushed too far, her body didn't have the energy.

"Lily? Lily?"

"Lily?!"

Two voices were calling her, Jeremy, and she thought Ben, but she had no breath to answer. She was slowing, her breath cramping. Coming from somewhere to her right, they were still too far away. She wasn't going to make it. Around her, the leaves were getting stronger; she could feel their pull like an undercurrent. An undercurrent that would drag her down, into its dark, decaying depths and drown her.

She was staggering now, her legs so tired she was unable to feel her feet, as if she were moving on the stumps of her ankles. A beech tree lay just ahead. Huge, its trunk almost a metre wide and its limbs heavy, it towered over her. The ground around it had fallen away into a small hollow, leaving the roots open to the air, arched like the legs of the spider. Stumbling around it, she heard a deep rumble, the ground shook, and out of the corner of her eye she saw a root pull back, retracting, like a finger. It caught her foot, tipped her forward and she fell, plunging headlong, with a loud cry of terror.

She hit the ground hard, her splayed body sliding through the leaves, sending them upwards in clouds of dancing, fluttering yellow, red and brown. Shocked, for a moment, she lay still, but feeling them ripple beneath her, she climbed onto all fours, then back to her feet.

To her left, an oak tree sat on top of an upward sweep, the ground around it raised and sloping, like an island in a sea of leaves. And without thinking, she scrambled upwards and, half-crawling, half-staggering, desperately threw her body towards it.

Reaching the tree, she pressed her hands to the trunk and, pulling herself around, sank down, her back against the trunk. Beneath her, its semi-exposed roots fanned out, like the raised veins on the back of an old's woman's hand. Panting, feeling like her heart was going to burst, she knew it was only a brief reprieve. The tree's limbs were too high to climb, and there was no sign of Jeremy or Ben. No sound of their voices, calling. Just her own ragged breath and the hard, dry rustle. Maybe the voices had been in her head, her imagination playing tricks on her.

Without meaning to, she slipped down until she was half-sitting, half-lying against the trunk of the oak, her breath whistling through her chest. Already, the leaves were coming for her. Slipping over one another, their numbers growing and swelling, as they slid across the ground towards her.

Exhausted, her energy spent, she gazed up into the dark, almost empty branches and, listening to the creak of wood, and the low, quick rustle, waited for them come.

It wasn't long. Nuzzling at her shoes, like animals, they slid over the tree roots and onto her feet, making her skin crawl. Part of her knew she should fight, should leap up and kick them from her, but she had nothing left. Even if she had, if she managed by some small miracle to clamber into the tree, away from them, she knew there was no point. It wasn't the leaves. They weren't alive. It was the Green Man, and he was everywhere, the embodiment of the whole forest. And she was lost, alone, in the centre of it.

The leaves were up to mid-thigh. But more were coming, sliding, piling on top, their combined weight pushing and pressing. It was like being eaten alive by a giant snake, feeling the press of its jaws as, millimetre by millimetre, its mouth worked up and around. That thought did it. Dragging up her last reserve from somewhere deep, she put down her hands and tried to pull herself up, out of their grasp, but her legs wouldn't move. She tried again, but the leaves swarmed her hands, tickling her skin with their rough, dry edges. Snatching them away, she fell back, her head resting on the smooth bark. Beneath her, the ground trembled slightly. It trembled again as the tree roots began to inch sideways and spread like tentacles, making way for her body in soft, loamy earth. She thought she heard Jeremy calling her again, but she'd been tricked before. For she realised now, it wasn't her head, but the forest that had tricked her, sending her away from the others and onto a different path. No, there would be no Jeremy, no Ben, appearing at the last minute to rescue her. This was the end and, with no way out, she accepted it.

The ground was falling in beneath her, dropping into the gaps left by the roots. She was falling with it, her head and shoulders slipping from the tree as her body slid into the earth. She thought idly of struggling, of pulling herself upwards, but she couldn't seem to focus. As if the heady scents of the forest, the mulch and the mould and the dark, dark soil, were soporific, lulling her silently to sleep.

The leaves were on her chest, their numbers continuing to swell. Pressing down, her lungs felt cramped; it was hard to breathe. Gasping for the last precious bits of air, she closed her eyes.

Something dropped onto her face, tickled her nose, then fell away. Opening her eyes, she looked up. Swaying gently back and forth, a leaf was dropping downwards. More followed, the last of the oak tree's canopy, she realised sleepily, falling, like tears. As if the tree was crying for her.

And then she saw it; in one single moment of clarity before her death. This forest was home to thousands, millions, of life forms, a colony, a vaulted, green, cathedral-like city. She knew all this, and yet, she'd never thought of it before, never really noticed. The woods and forests were just somewhere pleasant to walk, to be surrounded by nature, in the beautiful, lush quiet. As if it was made for her, and the people like her. But it wasn't. It wasn't made for any of them.

The leaves were at her chin; everything but her head was covered, and, strangely, she was no longer afraid. This city was a fraction of what it once was. A glimpse, a whisper of the giant forests that had covered this land. And would it be so bad to lie here, warm, cocooned, with the soft, sweet scent of earth in her nostrils, until she died? There were worse places to end your life.

Her eyes closed, her mind drifting. She was a kid again, on a field trip at primary school, sitting in a field on the edge of the woods with the sun on her shoulders. And a pencil in her small, podgy hand, holding it in a fist, tracing and drawing leaves.

Chapter Seven

Someone was yelling, their voice high and frantic, the sharpness penetrating the deep recesses of her brain. The image of the sunlit field vanished, and she heard movement above her, felt the leaves being pushed and knocked from her. Hands caught her face, neck, and chest, and she sensed more than saw arms swinging.

"Lily! Lily!"

It was Jeremy. He'd found her. At that moment, she knew she was dead. It was the only answer. Last minute rescues only happened in films.

"Ben, help me! Get her out."

They pulled at her arms and shoulders, dragging her out. Air hit the back of her throat, and she coughed, choking.

"That's it. Easy does it."

She felt them duck down, place their heads under her arms, and lift. Her chest heaved. Moved in and out, as her lungs sucked in precious air, and she opened her eyes. Bent close, Jeremy was to her left and Ben to her right. All she could see was one side of their faces, an eye each and the side of their nose. Jeremy's was flecked with red, and from this angle, Ben's looked larger than it did from the front. She was wrong; she couldn't be dead, she decided, staring at it. How would she know that about Ben's nose?

They were moving her, her feet dragging, churning the leaves, making them crackle and rustle. Her heart jumped, for a moment; she thought it was going to start again, but beyond their feet the leaves were still, unmoving. The Green Man had gone. She could sense his absence, suddenly, feel it in the forest's green calm.

"Over here," Jeremy said, steering them to a massive, low tree stump, all that was left of a felled horse chestnut.

They lowered her gently until she was sitting on the stump. Then Jeremy slipped down next to her and placed his arm around her, as if to hold her up.

"Lily, Lily, are you okay?" he asked.

Her head on his shoulder, she considered his question carefully, her mind working in slow motion. Even now, she wasn't totally convinced that this wasn't a hallucination, a last gasp of her dying brain. And if it wasn't, she had no idea if she was okay or not; she felt too dislocated, as if her body wasn't really hers.

"Yes, I'm alive," she heard a voice whisper hoarsely. Was that her?

"You're what?!" Confused, Jeremy looked at Ben then back. "Yes, I know you're alive." He laughed, throwing his other arm around her and pulling her close.

He was crying. Not much, just a few drops, but she could feel them as he pressed his face tight to hers. The tears seemed to bring her back to herself, as if she were a sleeping, dreaming Snow White. Maybe it was the wonder of it; the thought that even after all this time, he still loved her that much.

"Jem." She slipped her arms under his, and they held each other.

"What happened?" he asked, into her ear.

She pulled away. "I can't…please, I want to go."

"It's okay." Another glance at Ben. "Do you think you could stand?" he asked, after a moment.

"I think so."

Her breath was settling. Her throat and chest felt sore, raw, and her whole body ached, but she couldn't expect them to carry her out. She was going to have to walk. Springing forward, Ben helped him to pull her up. She looked down at the leaves beneath her feet and shuddered.

"Are you okay?" Jeremy asked anxiously, still holding her arm.

Without the Green Man, they were just leaves, she reminded herself, taking a step.

"I think so," she said again.

Jeremy let her go, and she hobbled around in a small circle. Her legs were so stiff it was hard to get them moving, but she knew it would get easier. The two men were watching her intently. She looked at Ben's face, the frown between his eyes. It was such a relief to see him, and know he was alright. A thought occurred to her.

"Where's Amelia?"

"Amelia?" Ben asked.

Jeremy paled. "Oh, God, I— I forgot all about her…I heard you yell, and I didn't think…all I thought about was you."

"What are you on about?" Ben demanded, looking from

one to the other. "Amelia's not here. She went home."

The fear was back, not for herself, but for Amelia. "No, Ben. She's here. She came with us. To find you."

He shook his head. "No, she can't be. I would've seen her."

"She was ahead," Jeremy explained quickly. He looked terrible, his face a mixture of horror, dismay and a slow, burgeoning guilt. "But when she went around a corner…I followed, but I couldn't see her, and then I realised I'd lost Lily as well, so I started back, and then I heard her shout."

Ben's face twisted as the full realisation hit him. "But then…she's in here, all alone!" He took a step back. "No, not Amelia…We have to find her!"

He turned away, opened his mouth to shout, to call for her, just as a scream pierced the air, thin with terror.

"Amelia!" Ben cried, bolting. "Amelia!"

He ran in the direction of the scream, his long legs sprinting. It came again, echoing through the trees.

"C'mon!" Jeremy shouted, darting forward.

A few paces, and he stopped and waited. He wouldn't leave her. Hobbling, going as fast as she could, she joined him, and the two of them went after Ben.

Already he was far ahead, weaving through trees. They were going to lose him. They sped up, Lily pushing her legs and their awkward, rolling gait into a half-run. Another scream, much closer, from somewhere off to the right. It was guiding them back, Lily realised, into the dense part of the forest she'd run out of. Was that what the Green Man had been doing? Using her to lead them away from his real target?

"Amelia!" Ben shouted, turning right and diving between two trees.

They could hear him crashing through the undergrowth.

"This way," Jeremy cried.

Grabbing her hand, Jeremy pulled her with him, into the thick vegetation. They went diagonal, cutting across the forest, to try and make up the lost ground. With Jeremy in front, pushing and shouldering the low-lying branches and bush aside, he made it easier for her, but she was still slowing him down. Ben shouted again, sounding closer. They were gaining on him, but too slowly, and Lily was tiring; she didn't think she go much further.

Veering left suddenly, Jeremy tugged hard at her, almost pulling her off her feet, and she stumbled, would've fallen, if his hand hadn't kept her upright.

"Sorry. Okay?" he asked, glancing back, his eyes wide.

She nodded, not having the breath to answer. They couldn't lose Amelia. Not now, not after everything.

"Amelia! Amelia!" Ben's voice shouted, sounding even closer. "Christ…somebody help me!"

He'd found her. Her heart beating wildly, Lily peered past Jeremy and into the trees, but there was no sign of Ben. He was still too far away.

Seconds passed, slipped into minutes. Still pushing through the undergrowth, they could hear him shouting frantically, calling to Amelia, his voice getting louder and louder. And now they could hear another voice, crying and pleading for help.

"Ben!" Jeremy yelled. "Where are you?"

"Here! We're here!"

With another sudden spurt of energy, Jeremy pulled on her, forcing her to match his pace. He veered left again, around a bush, then all but dragged her into a glade and stopped.

Ben was there, tugging and pulling on the branch of a tree. "Help me!" he cried, seeing them. "Help me get her out!"

Lily couldn't move. Rooted to the spot, she could only stare in horror as Jeremy dropped her hand and ran over to help him.

In the centre of the glade sat a circle of trees. Tall, their half-empty branches stark against the fading light, there was something almost human about them. As if they were ancient druids gathering, dark and ominous in long black cloaks, or a midsummer wedding party, turned by the devil not to stone, but living, growing wood.

Behind them, the floor of the glade was a mess. Holes dotted the ground; wide, imperfect circles where the soil had fallen in or been dragged upwards. Lines radiated out from them, towards the circle. Deep cuts that lifted the soil, raised it up like raw, angry welts on skin. As if someone had ripped out the trees then reached down for what was left of the roots and pulled. Or worse, the trees had simply pulled up their roots, like old-fashioned women lifting their skirts, and moved themselves. Lily shook her head; it wasn't possible. Trees didn't move.

Each tree anchored by the central root left in the soil, the smaller roots had lifted up and out. Then snaked along the back of the trunks, meeting one another and entwining. The side branches and twigs had slipped sideways too and, stretching out and reaching, had crossed and recrossed until they'd created a thick, wooden mesh that covered the gaps between the trees. She could hear the branches creaking as they slid across one another, stretching and tightening.

Trapped inside, Amelia was no longer calling out, but Lily could hear her sobbing.

Grunting with the effort, Ben and Jeremy were tearing at the branches, pulling at the small branches and the twigs, trying to bend them back or break them to make a hole. Jeremy twisted a twig, and the fibres split then broke. Quickly, he moved to another, but with a loud creak, two branches stretched out, covering the gap. But by moving across, the branches had left another, albeit smaller, one.

"Lily, don't just stand there! Help us!" Jeremy shouted, glancing back.

And then she saw it. Over his shoulder, peering out of the trees on the edge of the glade, was the face of the Green Man. Its mouth open, its eyes glaring as they bored into the back of Ben's neck, even from here she could see the movement of the vine between its teeth. Suddenly, she knew what to do, and the certainty released her. Turning away from them, she moved away, towards the other side.

"What are you doing?!" Jeremy cried, incredulous. "Lily! We need you here!"

She ignored him. Two metres from them, and out of sight, the gaps were slightly bigger here, as if the trees were spreading their branches the other way, focusing on protecting the area of the men's attack. Stepping in close, she began pulling at the smaller branches, twisting them just like Jeremy had done. Bits dropped away, making the gap bigger. She could see Amelia on the other side. Lying on the ground, almost completely buried by leaves, only her shoulders, neck and face were visible. Lily worked faster, pulling, tearing and twisting as hard as she could. The hole was growing.

"Lily, we need you!"

"I'm helping!" she yelled back. "You two stay together. And whatever happens, don't stop!"

Lying in the centre of the circle, Amelia's eyes were closed, and her blonde hair spread out beneath her head, like a pillow, as if she were already prepared for death. There wasn't much time. She pulled at long, brown branch, pointing upwards, and it broke off with a snap. Rotten. Tossing it away, she grabbed the branch above it. Another snap. The tree was half-dead, she thought excitedly; another one and maybe she could squeeze through. Pulling it out, letting it drop, she went for another.

The trees behind her rustled, and she turned. It was there, glaring at her, the vine in its mouth, turning and turning. Behind her, branches creaked as they rushed to cover the hole.

"That's it," she muttered. "Focus on me."

Ben began to swear, to shout and to rant. "Fuck you! Let me in. Let me in!"

She heard a loud bang, and a tree on the other side shook, scattering leaves. Another bang, then another. It was Ben. In desperation, he was kicking a low branch, over and over, making the whole mesh shake.

A loud crack ripped the air, the sound echoing.

"That's it!" Jeremy yelled, excitedly. "Do it again!"

Ben had broken a branch. They were both kicking it now, the whole frame shuddering. She had to be quick. She didn't know if this would work, but if it did, surely it would buy them the time they needed. Stuffing her hand into her pocket, she pulled out Marjorie's lighter and, wrapping her fingers around it, in a fist, covered it with her other hand.

"I know what you are, what you're made of," she said to

the Green Man, trying to hold its attention as she moved towards it. "And you won't take her. We'll get her out."

Its marble eyes bored into hers, rolling and burning with hatred. As if in anticipation, the vine was turning faster, the sap sliding off the lips and trickling down onto its chin.

Not far now. Keeping the lighter covered, she readied her hand, getting her fingers and thumb into position. She was lying; she didn't know, but if it was the embodiment of the forest, surely it would react to fire?

She heard another crack. A flurry of activity behind her, and as the rolling marble eyes turned to look, she leapt.

"Go, go!" Jeremy shouted at Ben.

Throwing her arm forward, she spun the wheel with her thumb and pressed. A rasp of flint and the flame caught and, with a wild shout, she thrust the lighter hard into its face.

There was no sound. No supernatural shriek or scream. She saw pain in its eyes, smelt the faint scent of wood burning, and the turning vine slowed, then stopped. The Green Man's lips closed. For a split second, they gazed at one another, and then it was gone, disappeared into the forest. The flame extinguished and, feeling strangely guilty, as if she'd been forced into killing an attacking animal, she lowered her hand.

"Amelia! Amelia!"

Ben was inside, pulling, dragging her body out of the leaves. Darting around the circle, Lily saw Jeremy leaning into the circle through a gap in the branches.

"Hurry up. Get her out before it comes back!" she yelled, coming to join him.

Unmoving, as Ben held Amelia's body up, Jeremy took one of her arms and began to back out.

"Lily, take the other one," he grunted, his face bathed in sweat.

Stood together, as Ben lifted and eased her out, they took more of her. Unconscious, she was heavy and, with an effort, they lowered her gently to the ground. Leaves clung to her, lay tangled in hair.

"Is she okay?" Ben asked anxiously, clambering through the gap.

On her knees beside her, Lily bent her face to Amelia's.

"She's not breathing." She looked at Jeremy.

"Lily, you've done mouth-to-mouth." He joined her on the soft, damp soil.

"That was years ago."

And they had to get out of here, before the Green Man returned. But there was no choice. Amelia wasn't breathing. Rocking back on her heels, she wiped the hair off her face.

"Think, Lily, think," she told herself, even as she glanced back, into the trees, looking for the Green Man.

She forced herself to focus. She was back in the classroom, at the college, with a group of local volunteers, trying to resuscitate a dummy. "First thing; check the airway."

With Ben hovering, she opened Amelia's mouth to its fullest and, crouching down, peered inside. Nothing in there; no leaves. Just to make sure, very gently, she placed a finger inside. No nothing.

"Now, tilt the head back," she muttered, remembering. "Forehead and chin."

It was coming back. Reciting the instructions in her head, she placed her left hand on Amelia's forehead and, with the other, pushed her chin, opening the airway. Then, getting into position, she began the chest compressions. She counted thirty, then, pinching Amelia's nose firmly, she breathed into her mouth, once, twice, each time making sure her chest rose. She began the compressions again.

"It's all my fault," Ben said bitterly. Placing his hand on his head, he turned away and began to pace.

She did the whole thing again. Ben was still pacing. One hand rubbed his hair, while the other pressed his stomach. He looked, then looked away again, as if he needed to watch, but couldn't bear to.

Again. "One-two-three…" Lily counted.

"I think she's breathing," Jeremy said suddenly, eagerly.

Lily stopped. Dropped her hands and looked. He was right. Amelia's chest was lifting and lowering all by itself. She was breathing. She sat back, and for the first time, noticed how dark it was getting. Both Ben's and Jeremy's faces were streaked with shadow.

"Is that it? Is she alright?" Ben asked, dropping his hand, and coming close.

"She's breathing. But we need to get her to a doctor."

"Should we move her?" Jeremy asked.

"Do we have a choice?" she countered, with another glance at the trees. "It's getting dark, and we have to go before it comes back."

"I'll carry her," Ben interjected, calm, determined, now there was something for him to do.

Bending down, he picked her up then, straightening, cradled her to him, her head on his shoulder, as easily as if she were a small child.

"Which way?" Jeremy asked, looking around.

"This way," Ben replied, already moving.

He was heading out of the glade in a completely different direction. Jeremy and Lily looked at on another.

"Are you sure?"

"It's all coming back," he replied over his shoulder, not turning. "We knew this wood as kids. There's a road and a car park. They're not far."

Joining him, Jeremy darted forward, going ahead so he could clear the way for him, while Lily brought up the rear. Minutes passed, and the only sounds were the noise they made pushing through the undergrowth and their breathing. Once, twice, Lily glanced back, but there was no sign of the Green Man. After what she'd done, was it possible that it would let them go so easily?

The wind was picking up. She could feel it, passing through the forest, with the faintest of shivers. But now the trees were thinning. Another minute, and they stepped out into another long, open sweep of forest.

Dark against the fading light, their limbs twisted with age, their trunks made bulbous with canker, the trees were grotesque, like something out of a nightmare. Giant shadows stretched away from them, filling the forest floor with darkness. Crunching and rustling, they walked across the leaves. Passing under trees, they moved from brown to black and back again, stepping on shadows. It was like the childhood game of giants Lily and her older sisters had played. Step on their shadow and you freeze them, stop them from moving. But step off their shadow and they're free to come get you.

She looked up, into the branches of the trees. Behind them was the last of the sky's light. The sun was setting. Giants.

Only six or seven, the game had terrified her, but never in her worst nightmares had she imagined that the giants who came after you could be trees.

The wind blew again. Stronger, and cold, coming from the North, it swooped down through the trees towards them, catching branches as it passed and lifting and tossing the leaves before it. Lily's heart began to pound. It was here. She could feel it. Hear it creeping, coming closer, in the creak and the rustle.

More gusts, and suddenly, the wind was roaring, the violence of it taking them by surprise. As the trees above their heads shook, Ben staggered sideways, two small footsteps to his right, and he hefted Amelia, pulling her close.

"Where did that come from?!" Jeremy shouted.

"It's not far!" Ben shouted back.

The ground began to slope upwards. Shrieking, the wind battered and pummelled at them, as if trying to force them backwards. Around them, the whole forest was dancing. Shaking, screaming, creaking, and roaring, like Woden's frenzied Wild Hunt. They bent their backs, pushing against it, and then the rain hit.

Torrential, they were drenched in seconds.

"Almost…there," Ben breathed.

"I see, look!" Jeremy shouted, pointing straight ahead.

A light flashed through the trees, going fast. A car! They were almost there. Digging deep, Lily swung her arms, using them to help propel her like the oars in a boat. Almost there. She could see the gap in the trees.

Stifling a groan, Lily was almost bent double, trying to force her body forward. Slipping and sliding across the wet leaves, Ben was already through, Jeremy going next. She was just a metre away.

Even in the wind, she could hear voices, the faint murmur of chat. People. A tree creaked to her left. A small oak tree that still had most of its leaves. Even as she looked, the leaves lifted and parted, revealing the face of the Green Man.

It stared straight at her, ignoring the others. Its mouth closed, on one side of its face was an oval-shaped dark brown stain, ringed with black, where she'd singed and burnt it. The marble eyes rolled, giving her flashes of red, orange and gold in amongst the brown and green. One more step and she was out of the wood and onto the road, safe. She stopped.

From here, she could see the car park was across the road, metres to the left. A car was coming out, indicating right, its lights blurred by the rain. Behind it, she could see two more cars, and people, a couple, and an old man with a dog, walking swiftly towards their cars.

"Hello, we need help!" Jeremy shouted, waving his arms and breaking into a half-run.

The car pulled away, the driver staring, but he didn't stop. Behind, standing next to their cars, the others had stopped and were staring too. Spotting Amelia, and ignoring the rain, the woman said something to her partner, and the two rushed forwards. Hugging the side of the road, watching for car lights, Jeremy and Ben went to meet them.

Lily and the Green Man stared at one another. Rain trickled down its face like tears. There was something in its eyes, something new. It was pain, she realised, from the burn she'd inflicted.

"I'm sorry," she said softly.

No response. She didn't know what she was expecting. But she'd only been defending herself. It had tried to kill her, and almost succeeded in killing Amelia. The eyes continued to roll. The hatred was still there, behind the pain. Next time, the eyes seemed to say, when you come back, and you will, I'll be waiting.

"Lily? Lily?"

Jeremy was calling her. Glancing over, she saw Ben placing Amelia in the back of the couple's car. She looked back at the Green Man, but it had gone.

Chapter Eight

The phone was ringing. Curled up on the sofa with a blanket, Lily lifted her head but, thinking it might be Ben, Jeremy was already there.

"Hello? Anthony! How's things?"

She heard him move off, into the kitchen, and wondered if he'd tell him what happened. Probably not. They might be close, but not even Anthony would believe him. No one would – no one could. Not unless they'd seen it with their own eyes.

The couple and the old man had been amazing. After a quick discussion, the couple (Tom and Julie) had taken Ben and Amelia straight to A and E, while Walter drove Lily and Jeremy back to their car. Thinking on his feet, Jeremy told them Amelia had tripped and fell, and they had no reason to doubt it, although Walter had given Lily a strange look when she'd all but crawled out of his car and hobbled over to their own. As if he was wondering how she'd got into such a state.

Lily sighed. She was so tired, but she couldn't sleep. They'd found Ben in A & E, sat in the waiting area, his head in his hands.

"They said I had to wait here," he told them. "They're doing tests. Whatever that means."

"Did they say anything?" Lily asked, carefully lowering her body into the seat next to him, trying not to wince.

He shook his head. "Not really. She did wake up in the car, though."

"Did she?" Jeremy exclaimed, still standing. "That's good, isn't it?"

"I guess," he agreed glumly. "But it wasn't long. A few seconds."

"It doesn't matter. She woke up, that's the important thing." Jeremy insisted.

Ben nodded. "I called her parents, they're on their way," he said after a moment. "I should never have gone there. This is all my fault."

Lily touched his arm. "No, Ben, it's not yours, it's mine. If I hadn't wanted the big story, if I hadn't pushed you, or found out about Sally Longmate, you wouldn't have gone back and none of this would have happened."

"I suppose," he agreed halfheartedly.

Silence.

"But I'm glad I destroyed my work," he said suddenly, the look in his eyes ferocious. "It's like it was feeding off it. Getting stronger and stronger. I never want to draw again."

"Don't say that!" Indignant, she pulled herself upright, and the look her eyes was no less ferocious. "Ben, you have such talent. You can't stop."

He shook his head. "You said the best bit about my work was the anger. But that wasn't me, it was…y'know. None of it was me."

"But it was you, don't you see?!" She flapped her hand irritably. "That's what artists do, isn't it? Convey what's already there. But seen through your eyes, your thoughts, your… soul. Didn't you tell me almost exactly the same thing?"

"But why did it choose me? I didn't want…any of it."

"I don't know. Maybe it didn't choose you. Maybe it's just that you can see it. Like me. Maybe not everyone can."

Instinctively, she glanced at Jeremy. He hadn't seen it, hadn't even known it was there.

Ben didn't answer. Head down, he seemed to be listening, but she wasn't sure if anything she said was going in.

"Ben, you can draw, paint anything. You said you tried, but you kept coming back to forests – maybe that was because of the trauma buried deep inside you. But now it's all out in the open, and you've faced it, it'll be different. You'll be free of it. Surely it's worth a try, before you give up on everything you've worked so hard for?"

"I guess," he repeated, not lifting his head.

"Ben." He looked up. "I believe in you. You saved Amelia; you can do this."

Gazing into his eyes, she said it with all the conviction she could muster. She owed it to him. Looking away, he laughed awkwardly.

"You'll try?" She knew she had him.

"Yeah, I'll try."

"And let me know."

Another laugh, this one more natural. "Yeah, I'll let you know. At least now I know it's not just me; you saw it too."

To her surprise, he took her hand and held it between his.

"Yeah, I saw it too," she smiled. "You're not alone

anymore, Ben. Whatever happens, whatever you do, you'll know it wasn't you."

A nurse appeared, walking swiftly towards them.

"Ben?" she asked, looking straight at him.

"Yeah."

"Amelia's awake, and asking for you. Do you want to see her?"

Letting go of Lily's hand, he jumped up. "Is she okay?"

"We're still awaiting the results of the tests, and until then, the doctors won't say." She flashed him a smile. "But she's awake and talking, so that's a very good sign."

"We'll wait here," Jeremy said quickly, slipping into the vacated seat.

"Yeah, okay."

A quick, distracted glance back, and then he was gone, scurrying after the nurse.

*

Lily needed the toilet. Reluctant to move, she'd held on too long. Throwing off the blanket, she got painfully to her feet.

"Aw, aw, aw."

Somehow, saying it out loud seemed to help. She'd never been so stiff before. Even the hot shower when she'd got home hadn't helped. Supposed to relax and ease her muscles, if anything, it had just made them throb even more.

She hobbled out into the hallway and, one hand on the bannister, began slowly to climb the stairs. On the phone, Jeremy exclaimed loudly, the sound echoing out from the kitchen.

*

Amelia's parents had arrived about ten minutes later. Rushing straight to the desk, Lily and Jeremy had only known it was them when they asked for Amelia. Not sure whether to approach, worried that introducing themselves would only make things worse, they'd stayed back. They were still debating when Ben reappeared. A few words with Amelia's mum and dad, and he led them into the medical area.

"Did you see the way Amelia's father looked at him?" Jeremy said.

"Fathers and their daughters. His first instinct will be to blame Ben. My dad didn't like you at the beginning."

"He didn't?!" Jeremy's eyebrows lifted. "You never told me that before."

"He thought you were a privileged posh boy who'd get me pregnant then make a run for it."

"But I wasn't posh! And you were in your early twenties. I mean, you weren't exactly a kid, and I definitely wasn't your first!"

She ignored that. "You were to him. Your dad had a good job, and owned his own house, which was quite big, to be fair."

"Yeah, only because he renovated bit by bit. You know they'd never have been able to afford it otherwise."

"I know." She smiled at him affectionately. "Even after all these years, you still don't get class, do you?"

"What?! Lily Goodfellow, art critic for a Sunday paper, seen at all the top galleries, quaffing expensive wine, lecturing me on class?!"

They smiled at one another.

"How you doing?" he asked then, touching her hair lightly.

"I'm okay. You?"

"Fine."

They joined hands, stroking fingers. They were both lying – after what had happened, neither of them was okay, but Lily thought that in a few days, or maybe even longer, when the memories had faded a little, they would be.

*

Coming out of the toilet, Lily looked at the door of their bedroom opposite. Closed, she pushed it open and, without turning on the light, went over to the window. The streetlights shone in the darkness, illuminating the street and path around them and one side of the trees. Without meaning to, she found herself staring at the tree nearest.

It was just one tree, one of the many planted on both sides of the street over a century ago. Not enough for a forest. She put her hand on the windowsill, using it to help keep her body upright. There was no Green Man here, no dark embodiment made ferocious with fury. It was just a tree that made the city street greener, more pleasant. A tree she passed every day, mostly without noticing. But what about the other forests, the other woods, the copses and the parks across the country, or the world? Would she ever be able to enter one again? Would any of them?

"Lily? Lily?" Jeremy was calling her.

She imagined him at the bottom of the stairs, his face turned upwards.

"Coming." She turned to go, but he was already bundling upstairs, so she waited instead.

"You off to bed?" he asked from the doorway. "Do you want the light on?"

"No, I'm coming back down in a minute."

He took a step towards her. "Are you alright?"

"Yeah, fine."

"It's just… I'm still talking to Anthony, but I wanted to check something with you." He stopped.

"O-kay."

"Anthony was telling me…he's met someone."

"Met someone?"

"Yeah. Her name's Gina. He's been seeing her for almost a month, and he wants us to meet her. He's invited us over on Saturday. What do you think?"

It seemed strange it was now, after all these months, when it was Marjorie's lighter that had saved them.

"Yeah, of course."

"But are you sure you're up to it, after…everything?"

"Yeah, it'll be nice."

It was a cliché, but Marjorie would've wanted Anthony to be happy. And would've wanted, no, expected, Jeremy and Lily to support him, no matter what.

"I'll let him know."

He disappeared, and Lily turned back to the tree. Life continued. Another cliché, but also true. And, hopefully, one day she'd feel okay to walk among the green, whispering giants with Jeremy, or Marjorie's lighter, kept carefully topped up, nestling in the bottom of her pocket.

It began to rain. Fine, misting, it wetted the street, making the tarmac and concrete gleam. The branches of the tree glistened spookily. Perhaps the forests had always taken some, but after all the cutting, burning and chopping, the clearing and eviscerating, it had become something more. Justice, maybe, or vengeance. But not too much, not too many, just in case the humans took their own revenge and erased what was left of it.

A man went by, walking two bulldogs that pulled and strained on their leads. Ben had interpreted his work through climate change, and it was hard for any sensible person to deny that, intentional or not, innocent or guilty, in the end, everyone was culpable. But what if there were others? Gods or sprites or demons, or whatever you called them. Embodiments of other landscapes; rivers, seas, mountains and prairies, the knowledge of them handed down in stories legends, and fables? Maybe, Lily thought, gazing out into the night, she shouldn't be afraid of what they were doing to the planet, but what the planet will do to them. Of the fury they'd unleashed.

Discover Luna Novella in our store:

https://www.lunapresspublishing.com/shop